What the press says about Harlequin Romances...

"...clean, wholesome fiction...always with an upbeat, happy ending."
　　—*San Francisco Chronicle*

"...a work of art."
　　—*The Globe & Mail*, Toronto

"Nothing quite like it has happened since *Gone With the Wind*..."
　　—*Los Angeles Times*

"...among the top ten..."
　　—*International Herald-Tribune*, Paris

"Women have come to trust these clean, easy-to-read love stories about contemporary people, set in exciting foreign places."
　　—*Best Sellers*, New York

Goblin Hill

by

ESSIE SUMMERS

Harlequin Books

TORONTO • LONDON • NEW YORK • AMSTERDAM • SYDNEY • WINNIPEG

Original hardcover edition published in 1977
by Mills & Boon Limited

ISBN 0-373-02068-6

Harlequin edition published May 1977

Printed in U.S.A.

To Mary and Thomas Gates, who know and love
every bay and buff on our lovely East Otago coastline, this novel about an imaginary headland there
is affectionately dedicated.

The author wishes to record her thanks to Alma Chamberlain for her poem "Youth," and to the unknown poet who wrote "Farewell to a Little Boy" (source unknown). She thanks the *Australian Woman's Mirror* for permission to use an excerpt from "Candlelight" by A.N.I.C.

CHAPTER ONE

Too much had happened in too short a time. Faith Charteris felt as if heart and mind had been bludgeoned. Certainly, as the only child of elderly parents, she'd accepted as natural that she might be left on her own fairly early in life, but to lose both within the year had been devastating.

Perhaps it was worse because she'd been her father's secretary, working at home with him. After her mother died, Faith had thought Stephen Charteris's work as an author would have been the saving of him, because he'd always lost himself completely in his characters' adventures, but it was soon amazingly evident that the gentle Lucy had been the mainspring of his existence, and a vigorous, colourful personality had slipped out of life with an uncharacteristic simplicity.

At twenty-five losing one's parents wasn't the tragedy it could have been at fifteen. One could fend for oneself and she had no financial problems. This lovely house overlooking Hawke Bay on the east coast of the North Island of New Zealand had been so designed that it would convert easily into two flats. So Faith could live in the smaller and rent the other, thus retaining her parents' treasures garnered from the four corners of the earth.

Her mind, as always, automatically corrected that ... the treasures of her *adoptive* parents. Ah, *there* was the rub. *There* lurked the stab of pain. The sense of loss at their going was now shot through with a feeling of having been let down by the two people she loved most. Again her mind checked. Loved most? What about Glen?— Glen Tankerville? Even had her parents lived she'd have left home soon, married. Glen would now fill that gap in her life, be her nearest and dearest.

Faith made up her mind that if she and Glen weren't blessed with children they would adopt, even as Stephen and Lucy had done, but those children would know from their first consciousness that they had been chosen, with love.

Certainly Stephen had written it out for her in the letter the solicitor had given her and it was expressed beautifully, as perhaps only such an artist with words could have done, but Faith knew, beyond all doubting, it had been the wrong way to handle it.

Worst of all had been the footnote, written just before he died, saying he'd written to her real mother to ask her to get in touch with her to explain the circumstances of her birth.

He'd said, 'I don't feel I can break the promise made her at the time, and reveal her name and your father's. But remember, darling, you've always been the child we desired, not only a daughter but a pal. Lucy said once that you were the child of her spirit. Mine too.' That had been true.

She'd thought Glen and his mother ought to be told, and told together. That had been a mistake, as she realised this very moment. Alone, he might have reacted swiftly, reassuringly, folding her to him and telling her it didn't, couldn't matter. Yet, because she'd sensed his mother wouldn't like it, she'd thought to spare him the telling.

Glen waited for his mother to speak first, as if he must take his lead from her. Well, of course he'd probably had a shock. He wasn't as warmly impulsive as Faith knew herself to be. It was foolish to expect the man one loved to be in exactly the same gear as oneself, especially one brought up by someone as reserved as Mrs Tankerville.

She was always described as a gracious, dignified woman, so her reaction was unexcited, completely un-

8

emotional. Also completely cold. Under the chill Faith sensed a decided withdrawal. She wasn't in the least concerned with the effect it might have had on the lonely girl before her.

Faith told herself it was no worse than she'd known it would be. There was no doubt Mrs Tankerville was proud of the fact that both she and the late Glendon Tankerville had united two of the earliest and choicest pioneer families of the Hawkes Bay province when they had married. Faith had been shown the family tree that went back to the Normans and it had been pointed out that his father's family had come from Tancarville in Seine Inférieure.

Faith and her father had chuckled over the ring of pride in her voice and Stephen had said, 'What a good thing the Charteris family is clearly from Chartres. But don't show her our family tree, Faith. Ours is so frank . . . did you notice she didn't have any black sheep on that one? Do you think she'd had them expunged from the records? Every family has them. But there wasn't a single traitor among them, or any sign of one born on the wrong side of the blanket! Perhaps they were like the Vicar of Bray . . . whatsoever king reigned, they were on his side! Don't give her a copy of my next book to come out, whatever happens. Do you remember my using that quotation from that doctor's column in the local paper on heredity . . . "The man for ever boasting of his ancestry is like a potato, the best part of him being underground"?'

Now it wasn't so funny. As a Charteris she'd been most acceptable. As a nameless nobody she was quite different.

It might still have been all right had Glen let himself go on the way home, but he hadn't. He kept on with tiny, mosquito-like questions till Faith could have screamed.

Had her parents never let any hint drop? Hadn't she told him she'd been born in London? Was it possible they'd gone there with the express intention of adopting

9

a child and passing it off as their own? When did she think Stephen had written to her real mother? Had she any idea of her whereabouts? Could she have been English? How long did she think it would be before she would hear?

It was when he said, 'You *must*, of course, keep it entirely to yourself, apart from us, when and if she does,' that Faith swung round on him. 'Glen! You are taking it for granted, aren't you, that I *must* be a guilty secret in my mother's past?'

They were standing in Faith's entrance hall now. He hadn't let up all the way home.

Glen said in a tone so intentionally reasonable it was intensely irritating, 'Faith, you must face facts ... what other reason could there be?'

She swallowed, said, 'I admit it's hard to think of another, but I feel I must cling to some hope, Glen. Don't you see? Even if I am illegitimate, there may be extenuating circumstances. I mightn't have been fathered by some fly-by-night casual acquaintance. My parents may have intended to marry. My father may have been killed before he could marry my mother—that's happened more than once. There are plenty of worthy citizens about who, while they may not have been born out of wedlock, were conceived before their parents were married. That's no shame to them. My mother might even have been deceived, been a little too loving and trusting, perhaps too lonely. She may have wanted the best possible home for me, a name. And certainly I got that. Dad seemed to think, by his letter, that my mother wouldn't hesitate to respond when she knew both Lucy and he were gone. So let's wait and see.'

Glen said slowly, 'If she knows you don't know her identity she may never respond. She may have a husband and children who won't know about you. She may not want to be reminded of the folly of her past, may never *dare* acknowledge you.'

Faith gave a wounded sound. 'Oh, Glen, I've been trying to push that thought away, but hoped you'd tell me it didn't matter.'

He took a step towards her, but Faith visibly flinched. She wanted no tepid, meaningless kisses. Her upraised hand stopped him dead. 'Don't kiss me goodnight. I'm not giving to kissing when I'm not in a kissing mood.'

He stared. 'What an odd thing to say!' He looked affronted, resentful. To her great surprise that didn't worry Faith a scrap. She'd much rather appear unaffectionate than be the recipient of a too-formal parting kiss. Yet he could have battered down her defences by one step, one compelling embrace. But he recovered, said, with the air of one humouring a petulant child, 'You'll feel differently tomorrow, dear. It's been a strain telling us.'

'It certainly was. Much more so than anticipated.'

He took no notice of that. He looked thoughtful. 'I'd think your mother *was* English. She may not yet know of your father's—of Stephen Charteris's death. He only wrote to tell her he was near his end. Anyway, if she doesn't write, it will be for the best, I'm sure. No use raking up a doubtful past.'

Faith knew the distance between them widened with every word. 'Glen, I *must* know. Could you—given the same circumstances—bear not knowing the stock from which you sprang? It would be so different if I'd always known I was adopted, but to know Father has contacted my mother—Glen, could you bear it?'

He considered it, then, 'Faith, I find that hard to answer. I can't imagine myself in that situation.'

Something in Faith stilled, then died. Could anyone have such a lack of imagination? Had this happened to Glen, out of her love for him she'd have put herself in his place, suffered with him. She felt as if she'd never known him. She had a vision of him reading his newspaper, morning after morning ... accounts of tragic accidents, of sudden loss, frightening experiences, even murder. Would this man never think: How could I bear it if it happened to me, to someone I loved? No, he wouldn't. He'd never imagine himself in other men's shoes. Those were things that always happened to other people, not to the Tankervilles. Nor would he ever think: There, but for the grace of God, go I!

When she kept silence he said, 'You've no way of finding out if your mother doesn't write, have you?'

She'd worked that out for herself. She lifted clear discerning eyes to his. 'I have a way, Glen. Someone I feel might know, and whom I'm sure would tell me the truth. My godmother. I've already written to her.'

'Written to Philippa Meredith? Oh, Faith, was that wise? I know she's a wonderful person, but actors and actresses, by and large, aren't noted for discretion. She could talk, cause speculation. And why would *she* know? Oh, because she was present at your baptism, and was in London then. But would they have told her of your parentage?'

'Well, they knew each other so well. They were younger friends of her parents in Oamaru, though older than her. She was some time at the school of dramatic art— and they had two years in London about the time I was born.'

His eyes were thoughtful. 'H'mm. You could be right. Your mother might even have been one of that crowd. I mean that in the world of the theatre things——' He stopped, looked awkward.

'Do finish,' said Faith sweetly. 'I'm surprised you stopped.'

He said shortly, 'I don't want to hurt you.'

'You already have, earlier. So why spare me now? Go on, say they're a pretty loose-living lot. Oh, Glen, how can you lump people into categories? Even in this permissive age you get folk of high moral standards in all callings. People who prefer family life and constancy to cheap affairs and variety. I mean, look at Philippa and Mark. Never a breath of scandal, and their marriage is beautiful to behold!'

He still sounded forbearing. 'Faith, you'll feel a lot better after a good night's sleep. I'll see you tomorrow.'

She felt the prick of tears behind her eyes and subdued them. She had no intention of crying before him. She said instead, scornfully, 'What makes you so sure I'll get a good night's sleep? Anyway, goodnight. Don't lie awake worrying about *your* future, Glen. *I* won't mess it up for you. You've nothing to fear from me.'

He looked puzzled but turned to the door. Her voice arrested him. 'And Glen, it's just a small request, but it's one I hope you'll pay attention to.'

He looked apprehensive. She said, with anger, 'Just that you are never again to begin to say to me: ". . your father . . ." and change it to "Stephen Charteris." Not ever! Stephen and Lucy Charteris were my parents in everything but biological fact. My *dear* parents!'

He went without another word.

Faith made herself some coffee and cut some bread-and-butter. She laid a slice of cold chicken across it, spread it with mango chutney, bit into it with relish, and said out loud, 'Faith, I'm proud of you! You're not wilting. You're not going into a decline. You still have a jolly good appetite. It's just like that film Philippa starred in . . . Glen wasn't like the hero, *A Man to Ride the Water With.*'

It had been a Border film, and Philippa had been rescued from her hereditary enemies and had spent days being borne away on the hero's saddle-bow, through river and torrent, mountain and marsh. Faith could see her now, that luxuriant chestnut hair flowing out over her bodice and kirtle, the brilliant green eyes, the laughing mouth. She hadn't looked a day over twenty-one, yet she must be nearer fifty than forty, a magnificent actress, and an indulgent godmother.

The girls at Faith's High School had regarded Faith as favoured among mortals to have a television and film star for a godmother. She came to New Zealand once and had addressed the school assembly. The principal had chuckled. 'Not an absentee today ... boy or girl,' he'd remarked as he introduced Philippa Meredith.

Philippa hadn't glamorised her work at all, had spoken of the rigorous training, the physical and mental fatigue, the stamina one needed to throw oneself into parts, especially those of hers that called for daring, vitality, emotion.

Faith had glowed with pride at the way she'd brushed no one off for her autograph, how she'd singled out the shy ones, brought them out of themselves, had a special word for a fourth-former who was a little retarded, and had given a very generous donation to the school drama society. Not that Faith was a member. She'd been far more interested in the Literary Club, writing poems and short stories. She'd assumed, till a fortnight ago, that she'd inherited this as the daughter of Stephen Charteris. Wishful thinking, nothing more.

She'd cabled Philippa and Mark of her father's death. They had cabled back instantly, and there had been a magnificent floral tribute from them. It had been a long cable, but Faith had expected a letter to follow it. But there'd been nothing. There would be some good reason. Perhaps a letter had gone astray, which was more likely than that she'd not been able to make time. Even in the busy life she led, Philippa had been a wonderful correspondent.

Somehow warmed and comforted by the thought of Philippa and Mark, Faith slept dreamlessly till morning. Slept so long, in fact, that by the time she'd breakfasted, the mail had come.

She went out to the mailbox at the gate for it. The air was full of the scents of midsummer, January in New Zealand. All the flowers Lucy had so loved nodded from the borders, lilies of every description, from white, cool-throated ones, splashed with gold, to flaming tiger colours spotted with brown; roses of every hue and fragrance, the purples of buddleia and lassiandra, the flaunting loveliness of scarlet and pink hibiscus and along the green

14

turf that clothed half the street footpaths, were oleander blooms, reminding Faith of an Italian trip spent with her parents for the purpose of gen for a new thriller.

Her eyes swept the skyline, the dear familiar hills, the sea. Home. But now an empty, lonely home. She would never marry Glen Tankerville.

She reached in for the letters. Still more from readers of Daddy's books who'd just read of his death, a few business ones ... ah, an English airmail. She turned it over —yes, from Philippa. Typed, as always. She put the others on the letterbox, ripped this open. Philippa came to the point quickly.

'Darling Faith,
    You'll know all my heart would say, but I want to say it face to face. I would have flown straight out to you, had it been possible, but I just couldn't get away. Faith, air travel is so quick. Without a stop-over you could be with us in thirty-six hours. We'd like to pay your fare. You could be back in the same time if you need to for any unfinished business, after a good break with us. I'm tied up trying to finish a series. It would have been done long since had they not, for reasons I won't go into here, found it absolutely necessary to make a major change in it. Your father entrusted me with the task of revealing something to you—you'll know what by now—so I beg of you to come, and soon. Just send a cable to say when you'll be arriving. Stay as long a time, or as short, as you want to. You know Mark loves you even as I do. But come quickly or I might not be here ...'

Perhaps Philippa was off to Spain or Italy or somewhere for location filming. Or to Hollywood. Faith knew she'd go immediately. Her smallpox vaccination was still valid, so was her passport. It just remained to get a booking. She got out the car and drove down to the NAC office.

She was fortunate. She could leave on Friday. That would give her time to arrange some small details about the care of the house, pack and tell Glen. Tell Glen she was off to England and that she wouldn't marry him.

She did it gently, but with finality. He said, without any of his usual confidence, 'There wasn't a real need for this, Faith. I feel you're acting precipitately, not only in breaking things off but in going to England so suddenly. You could be told the details just as well by letter and it wouldn't be such a colossal waste of money.'

'How can anything that will give me peace of mind be a waste? Father and Mother would have wanted this. Besides, I might even be able to meet my real mother. With regard to the other thing, Glen, it won't cause you any embarrassment. As your mother said the other night, what a good thing we postponed announcing our engagement because of Dad's illness. She's not the only one to feel glad. I'm glad and grateful.'

'Why?'

'Because it showed me we weren't suited. I *did* love you, Glen, very dearly. So much so that had the positions been reversed I'd have only wanted to make it up to you. I couldn't risk marriage on those terms, Glen. If you failed me in this, the first test, I'd never have had confidence in you again. A girl has to be careful whom she picks for the father of her children. Her children might some day need the love and support of a man who could discriminate, recognise true values. Our children might have made mistakes, needed someone to help them, not condemn. I wouldn't risk it. You're no man to ride the water with!'

She wanted to laugh at the look on his face. This nameless waif was turning a Tankerville down! She wished she could cry when he left her. That would have been natural, but she knew why she couldn't ... she'd been in love with love, that was all ...

Now the big jet was dropping out of the sky over the

fields of England. There was the gleam of the Thames, the mass of Windsor Castle, the myriad trees, remnants of the great forests of other ages, still unspoiled ... lower and lower ... the multi-lanes of motorcars that crawled like ants along the network of roads came into view ... then the vast spread of Heathrow and touchdown.

She knew no great disappointment that Philippa wasn't there, because her free hours were always few, left over from her taxing studio work, and Mark was there instead, dear dependable Mark, so utterly unlike the preconceived idea of a film producer, never temperamental and tense. Yet, for once, he looked more finely drawn than usual.

When she'd kissed him she said, her fingers holding his chin so she could look at him squarely, 'Mark, you look awfully tired. Have you been overworking? Philippa mentioned a major change in this last series. Have you been working desperately against time?'

He nodded. 'Yes, love, just that. But it's over. What a good girl you are, travelling so lightly! Look, come on over here. A chap I know has put a room at my disposal. I wanted to brief you a bit and it's too hectic by far trying to chat while threading through the traffic on the Great West Road.'

Mark always knew someone. As they walked through the people thronging this hub of the universe, they said all the usual things ... how much sleep she'd had on the trip, how hot it had been in Los Angeles, what kind of a dawn had come up over Ireland ...

Then they were in the small interview room and Mark was closing the door. He came across to her, took her hands. 'Listen, Faith, I'm not going to try to break this gently ... we *have* been working against time. There *has* been a major change in the series, there had to be. Philippa had to be written out. The time that's been against us has been *her* time. She's got only a little while longer to live.'

Then he clamped his teeth down on his lower lip. Faith

freed her hands from his grip, slipped her arms about him, put her cheek against his in kindred, wordless sympathy. Then she said brokenly, because she somehow knew instinctively that her protestations would ease something for him, 'Oh, no, Mark! Not Philippa! She's so vital, so loved.'

They moved as one to a small settee against the wall, sat down, hands clasped.

He said, 'Oh, Faith, it's so cruel after your own loss such a short time ago. Your double loss ... because the day of Stephen's burial was the anniversary of Lucy's, wasn't it?'

She nodded, but said staunchly, 'Mark, my loss is nothing to yours. She's your wife. Is it certain it's terminal?'

'Quite certain. That's why she couldn't fly out to you when Stephen was ill. She was in hospital. We've known some time. She's fought gallantly—at first in secret. She was determined the series would write her out in the best possible way—not for her own glory, but because the livelihood of so many others depends upon it and if she could make it to a natural fading-out, there was the chance to bring in other characters to sustain it when she goes.'

'Oh, how like her, Mark! She's been so selfless all through her career, hasn't she? Never jealous of others, always helping someone to get a foothold, reach a good billing. She's been a legend in her own time. Mark, how long have we got her for?'

His lips were under control now. 'Not more than a few weeks. We finished her part in the series three days ago. It seemed as if she had the will to last out just that long. She had a reaction then, as we'd feared, but she's rallied because of your coming.' He looked at Faith. 'Would it be too much to ask you to stay till it's over? It would help her, I know.'

'Of course, Mark. No reason why I shouldn't—unless she'd rather have you to herself? Though I ought to be able to help with the nursing. I managed both Mum and Dad to the end.'

18

'She's counting on you staying.' He got up suddenly and went to the window, staring out unseeingly. He had the air of a man who doesn't know where to go from there.

She went across, touched his arm. 'Mark, I think you're worried about the fact that Dad laid it upon her to reveal to me my parentage. It may be too much for her —an awkward complication just now. What can we do about it? Can we make it easy for her? I've lived with it long enough now not to take on about it. I've faced all the possibilities and none of it need matter too much. I've twenty-five years of happy family life behind me.'

Mark's brown eyes, anxious and kind, searched the clear grey ones. 'Faith, it *is* your reaction to what Philippa has to tell you that's worrying me. At this stage so little could accelerate her passing, or make her last hours unhappy. She's determined to tell you herself, so I'm breaking faith with her, because I just dare not risk it.'

She had a line between her brows, puzzled. 'You mean you know who my mother is? Of course you do. She'll have told you in case she—died before I could get here. How like her. Then you just tell me—or leave it till—till after. Now this is happening to Philippa, I just won't have her upset. I'd like Philippa's last weeks to be as happy as we can make them. My mother's identity doesn't matter at a time like this.'

His grip was firm, compelling. 'Your mother's identity matters very much, Faith. It's going to be a shock, love, but—your mother was—is—Philippa herself.'

She had a terrific sense of shattering impact—and feared a black-out. Then her nails bit into Mark's palms and she rocked a little. Her vision blurred, but not with tears, and there was a singing in her ears.

Then everything came into focus again and reality had her in its hold. Her face was still devoid of colour, but she looked up into Mark's eyes and smiled. 'My mother, not my godmother! Oh, Mark, what a truly wonderful thing. I don't care what the circumstances were, it's still the most wonderful thing that ever happened to me. My mother is not a stranger.'

Mark had tears in his eyes and couldn't speak. Faith said, 'Philippa is, as I've just said, so unselfish. If I was the result of a time of foolishness, of loving too much, then of course she'd have had me adopted, to save me from suffering any stigma. Twenty-five years ago things were so different.'

Mark swallowed. 'Oh, bless you for saying just that ... but it wasn't that way at all. You were born in wedlock all right, for that matter conceived in wedlock, but ... Faith, there *was* a time in her heedless youth when she wasn't so unselfish. It seems to me that from that time onward when she realised how gravely she'd wronged your father—by marrying him—she disciplined herself never to be selfish again.

'Darling, what I'm telling you may be harder to understand than a woman giving up her illegitimate child—and you'd braced yourself to take that. Philippa was studying voice production in Christchurch. Your father was studying farming at Lincoln College near there. They fell madly in love and married. It just didn't work, couldn't. Julian's life was on the family's estate, he belonged to the fourth generation on that property. He thought she'd count the world well lost for love ... her acting career, in fact. He'd no idea, naturally, of her latent talent, of how compulsive it was, how burningly ambitious. But *she* knew it, so it was very wrong to marry him.

'Time drew near for Julian Morland to return to his farm. He'd gained his degree. Philippa wanted to come to London to study. They were just incompatible ... in their way of life. She walked out on him. She was only twenty-two, Faith. She planned it well, gave him no time to trace her before she left New Zealand. He'd gone down to the farm to prepare the cottage they were to have on the estate. She packed his things and sent them down to him, closed the flat, then wrote to him saying by the time he got the letter she would be on the high seas.

'When she reached London she found she was pregnant. To do her justice, she felt it wouldn't be fair to run home to Julian. He would have thought only necessity had driven her back to him. And she was sure their marriage wouldn't last. One day she met Stephen and Lucy in the Strand. She was so obviously pregnant and in such distress when she saw them, afraid they'd tell her folk, and pressure would be brought upon her to return, they promised not to disclose her secret. You can guess the rest.

'She'd been going to keep you, somehow. But Stephen and Lucy rented a house in Surrey, took her in, surrounded her with love, and you too when you came. They begged her to let them adopt you. She knew it would be a better life for you, that she'd see you from time to time, but she regretted it all her life. But she would never hurt the Charterises by demanding you back. Can you understand it at all, Faith? Understand and forgive?'

Tears were falling silently down Faith's cheeks. She brushed them away with the backs of her hands, as a child might have done. She nodded, then said, 'What of my father? Didn't he want to see me, ever?'

'He never knew. He still doesn't know. They were divorced, of course. She offered him his freedom, told him she'd never come back to him, that she just couldn't take his kind of life and it wouldn't be fair to him. She thought if he knew about you he might send for you. That if he married again, you might be an unwanted child, that she might never see you again. So she gave you to Lucy and Stephen.'

Faith nodded. That was more consistent with the Philippa Meredith she knew.

Mark said, 'Stephen and Lucy insisted you bore her maiden name as your first name, Meredith, so she could have some part of you. But in turn she asked that you be called by your second name. Faith is a family name on your father's side and in that first blissful year he'd said if ever they had a daughter, he'd like her called Faith.'

Mark continued, 'If you'd known the happiness your visits here with Stephen and Lucy gave her! She once gave up a part that carried a fabulous financial reward because it would have meant being out of London when they were bringing you over here. She was never jealous of your love for Lucy. It was something apart. She revelled in the fact that you loved her, not just as a god-mother, but as a person.

'I wish you could have seen the way she pored over photostatted copies of your school reports, your prow-ess in singing ... you got that from your father. Philippa, you'll remember, can't sing a note. She was glad you had his colouring, not hers, so that you wouldn't guess. Not that she wouldn't have been proud to claim you for her daughter, but because she thought it would hurt Lucy, who had been all the things to you that Philippa should have been.'

'I'm like my father?' cried Faith. She had a strange feeling sweep her ... she'd have liked to have rushed off to a mirror, to help her imagine that father.

'Mark, is he still alive? Does he still farm? And where?'

He smiled a little. 'That's my girl! He's quite a young man still, of course. He married again, a widow with a family, but has no children of his own. He farms on a small headland that juts out into the Pacific, some-where north of Dunedin. It's a curious formation, Phil-ippa says. It takes its name from that—Goblin Head. The homestead is called Goblin Hill. It's south of a place you sometimes see on New Zealand calendars, a place where the cliffs and shore have strange round boulders embedded in them that look like giant cannonballs. It's got a Maori name I can't pronounce. Know it?'

'Oh, Moeraki? We saw it once. Dad wrote a book about Otago and we called at Moeraki to see the builders.

How strange that I didn't know my forebears farmed near there.'

Mark said, 'Life compensated Julian. He made a very happy second marriage. His stepson runs the farm with him.'

'How do you know it was happy?'

He smiled broadly. 'Because he and his wife visited us here a few months ago. They were having a year off on a world tour. It was very courageous of Leonie, his wife. She came to see us unknown to Julian. Said she was sure Julian would like to meet Philippa again, but was afraid she, Leonie, wouldn't like it. She was so sweet. He'd gone to meet a farming group from NZ on tour here, and she came down to Surrey to see us. She rang us first.

'Philippa was so thrilled. I was staggered that she and Leonie took a genuine liking for each other. Philippa told her this had eased her conscience, that it had made her happy to think Julian had finally achieved the happiness he deserved. I think the fact that Leonie too had been married before helped.' He answered the question in Faith's eyes. 'No, she didn't tell him about you. She longed to, but Stephen was still alive. Darling, we must go. You can imagine how worked up she is, facing the moment of telling you. I lied to her—told her I'd rung the airport and your plane was to be an hour late. That gave me time to tell you, most of all, to see how you took it and to give you time to sort out your own feelings.'

Faith smiled at him, mistily. 'Let's go. I can hardly wait.'

Philippa Meredith had dressed, overcoming her weakness, then sent her maid out. Illness had aged her a little, but she still had that same shining look that so endeared her to audiences. Her green eyes were even more lustrous, the burnished hair was beautifully styled and the bone structure of her face was more exquisitely cameo-like than ever.

She knew immediately that Mark had told Faith. She looked apprehensive for a fleeting second as she rose, steadying herself by one hand, then Faith crossed swiftly to her, held out her arms, said, 'Oh, Mother, Mother, let's make the most of every precious moment!'

They had their month. They went down to the Denbys' Surrey house near Haslemere in an enchanted setting of beechwoods that were just misting greenly after their winter sleep. Philippa broke off a spray one day and touched the leaf-buds with loving fingers.

'So life goes on, spring after spring, always the sap rising in the trees, pushing off the old leaves, swelling the buds of the new. Oh, Faith, look ... there's the first snowdrop. Let's make a covenant, that you'll always think of me when you see your first snowdrop of the year? That will be the New Zealand September, of course. Will you, Faith?'

'I will, Mother. I'll never, never forget, and if ever I have a daughter, I'll tell her of this English spring day, and she'll teach her daughter to do it. She'll be so proud of her famous grandmother. We've created a tradition this day.'

Faith bent down, picked the snowdrop, said, 'I'll press this one and put it between today's pages of my diary.' She went on, 'It's not going to be easy watching you on television. Yet I couldn't bear not to watch you. We get ours later there.'

'Faith, my darling daughter, don't let the poignancy of that get at you too much. Please try to get joy, not anguish, out of seeing me. I can't help hoping that some-day in the future my old films will be dished up so that the children you'll have will be able to see their grand-mother.'

It was somehow given to Faith to control her tears when Philippa said things like that; to make the right rejoinders. It seemed as if Philippa's joy in having her daughter with her had superseded the pain they had expected, had triumphed over it.

Philippa said, 'When you marry, Faith, use your head as well as your heart. I think you'll have a happy life, because there's more of your father in you than of me. You have his stability. Your grey eyes are as steadfast as his, there's the same purpose in the lift of your chin. Those little curving lines each side of your mouth are his and his alone, and your brows, like his, darker than your light brown hair. But Julian's hair is grey now. The only thing you have of me is your laugh. Mark noticed it long ago.

'Faith, I'm so glad Leonie and Julian came when they did, before I showed any signs of illness. Oh, that's not vanity on my part, just that we were able to be a happy foursome, and Julian and I could both rejoice that we'd each, after much pain, found ideal partners. Wasn't Leonie brave? Because the screen has always glamorised me. But she has something I never had. It was marvellous that Mark and Julian got on so well together. It took away something of my guilt when we met, because Leonie, with her serenity and love of country life, had given Julian what I could never have given him. So perhaps in some way I'd injured him less by walking out on him.

'I didn't tell him about you because if he'd wanted to claim you, it would have hurt Stephen. Julian might so easily have wanted you, seeing that after four generations Goblin Hill must pass into the hands of those with no pioneer blood in them. But now Stephen is gone it can't matter. Child, would you like to see your father?'

Faith caught her breath. 'Mother, I just don't know. I've a natural curiosity, but as far as making myself known is concerned, probably not. It might disturb his life and Leonie's.'

'I understand. But I don't think it would, because she told me Julian was a good stepfather. So she'd be a good stepmother. But I've no rights in the matter, mustn't interfere. And if you did go south to Goblin Hill, it might seem very remote after the cosmopolitan life you lived with Stephen and Lucy.'

Faith said slowly, 'I suppose it must have been born in me to love the country life more than any. Remember how I used to spend all those holidays on my friend Judith's farm? I learned to muster, to dip, to act as fleecy in the shearing-shed even, to lamb the ewes, to dock tails. I used to say I must be a throwback to some unknown ancestor. Now I can say it's to my pioneer ancestors of Goblin Hill.' She paused. 'Mother, I'll do nothing hastily, but I might take a trip down south some time, ring them and say I was your goddaughter and you'd asked me to call if ever I was in the vicinity. Then, if it seemed to me the right thing to do, I might tell them. I'd play it by ear. How does that sound to you?'

'Wonderful! Bless you for thinking of it. I won't press for more. You have a wisdom I never possessed. Of course that's from Lucy's bringing-up. But if you do reveal your-self, I know Julian will love you. So will Leonie. She's sweet. And I feel I'll know, somehow, somewhere.' The brilliant green eyes looked past Faith's shoulder to the sunlight shining translucently through the frail green leaf buds of that Surrey hillside. 'Besides, you'll be in God's hands, my darling, and you'll be guided. Let's go back to the house now. I feel so content, so complete. Let's put this yellow jasmine in water. It's nearly over, but may give us a few days before these petals fall.'

Philippa was gone before the last petal fell to the polished wood of her windowsill. She died at sunset, lying back in a chaise-longue, propped up with pillows. 'I've always loved sunsets,' she said, on a whisper of sound so faint they knew instinctively that these were the last words they would ever hear her utter, and the next moment her breath was stilled.

Mark and Faith sat alone with their loved one for one hour of private grief. Because from then, till the last sad rites, she would belong to her public and the world of the theatre.

Faith stayed long enough to see Mark over the worst. She promised to come back later. He had so many true friends here, to help him. His work was exacting, so it would fill the hours; his widowed sister was coming from Scotland to keep house for him.

As he kissed her goodbye at Heathrow he held her tightly, said, 'Thank you for making her last few weeks so happy.'

As the big jet rose into the cloud-garlanded meadows of the sky, Faith knew a deep sense of fulfilment.

CHAPTER TWO

SHE knew exactly what she was going to do as soon as she reached home because she planned it all as she flew over oceans and continents and islands on the way home through the East.

She found tenants for the house, stocked up Stephen's motorised caravan with everything she could possibly need for a few months' travel round the South Island, sent off for an advertisement to the *Otago Daily Times* as soon as she had made a booking at a Dunedin motel.

It read: 'Typist-secretary, formerly employed by an author, seeks similar employment full or part-time in Dunedin or north of it. Very well versed in checking pioneer chronicles, museums, newspaper files, in editing and compiling. Would be interested in producing a centennial booklet or family history. Has own typewriter and tape-recorder and a caravan for personal accommodation if a country post is available. Apply Meredith Charteris, Robbie Burns Court Motels, Dunedin.'

She naturally hoped some country town near Goblin Head might be able to offer something. It was sparsely populated and even in, say, a forty-mile radius, she might be able to see and observe her father and his wife before calling on them as Philippa's goddaughter. Stephen's royalties would continue for long enough, so even if she got only a nominal fee for such work, it wouldn't matter.

Before leaving Napier she had something she must do. She felt she owed it to herself and to her mother. She went round to the Tankervilles, picking a morning when Glen would be at business. She was received with the famous graciousness that was no more than good manners, and lacked cordiality.

Faith sipped her tea, received Mrs Tankerville's polite regrets about her godmother's death. 'I expect she wasn't well enough to see much of you—pity, when it's so far and so costly. I expect you'd feel that under the circumstances you couldn't raise the question about your mother's identity?'

Faith's eyes lit up with such delight they looked almost blue. 'Oh, I didn't need to. Mark Denby, Philippa's producer and husband, told me at Heathrow. It was almost too wonderful to be true. Philippa Meredith *is*—was— my mother. And my father owns a sheep-station near Dunedin and doesn't even know of my existence. They married while they were both still students. Two years later I was born—but long before that Mother knew she'd made a mistake and left my father to go to a school of dramatic art in London. Before she got there she knew she was expecting me.

'Stephen and Lucy were friends of her parents, so they adopted me. My father and his second wife—a perfect darling—visited Mother and Mark just before Mother became ill.'

Mrs Tankerville pursed her lips, said thinly, 'It sounds a little too like one of the dramas Philippa Meredith acted on television.'

Faith drew from her bag her parents' marriage certificate. She laid it in front of Mrs Tankerville. In a few moments she left, knowing she had closed a chapter of her life.

She took her time going south, even dallying on the way in the North Island, before crossing to Picton on a car ferry, and then telling herself the indented coastline, two hundred miles long between there and Christchurch, was so enchanting she ought to take it in leisurely fashion. In her heart she knew it was because she was just a little afraid of taking on this venture. Afraid that the idyllic dream she had of being welcomed as a darling daughter might fall very short of fulfilment in actuality.

She had always loved Christchurch and for the first time had all the time anyone could want to explore it. Autumn was deepening into its full glory before she could tear herself away from it. Another two hundred miles to Dunedin, but before she would reach there, she would see the headland of Goblin Hill.

It was further on than Moeraki by quite a few miles, in fact between Palmerston and Waikouaiti. The signpost made her thumbs prick as it came into view. It said, 'Goblin Headland, No Exit.' The road dipped under the railway viaduct, then lost itself amidst a fine stand of native bush that clothed the gently-sloping shoulders of the headland for two-thirds of its height, then suddenly and dramatically from that bush reared the strange formation of rocks that did indeed look as if it were a petrified and recumbent goblin, beard, peaked cap and all.

Faith pulled in to the side of the road and lost herself in dreams. Here her forebears had come, in the very early days of the province, to wrest a living from the virgin soil. She gazed her fill, then drove on.

The caravan was driven into the motel parking-space, and she went across to the office. The owner smiled, and handed over a pile of mail. 'Looks as if your friends are all welcoming you to Dunedin. Good show! I'll take you to your unit now.'

Faith cooked her evening meal before examining the mail. She hadn't expected so many answers, and she'd feel better able to make a decision if she was fortified by food.

There was one from a firm who could do with a proof-reader-cum-typist ... well, that was in her own line and well paid at that, but right in the city. One was from a Central Otago newspaper—too far from Goblin Hill. Some were run-of-the-mill typing positions. The last one had an unfamiliar Maori name on the back of the envelope. It was East Otago. That was certainly the right area. Her pulses quickened. If it was at all suitable she'd take it. Money wouldn't matter. She opened it.

It was from two ladies, Mrs C. Fitzherbert and Mrs H. Pomeroy. Faith giggled. How Mrs Tankerville would have approved ... surely those names dated back to 1066! She mustn't expect anything too ideal though. But it was, it was.

'Dear Meredith Charteris,

When we saw your ad. in the *Times*, we felt it was truly an answer to prayer. For so long we've talked of compiling the family history. We have authentic records (in a shocking muddle, we must confess) of our family, who came out in the *John Wickliffe* in 1848, lived in port Chalmers and Dunedin at first, then took up land here. The MacIntyres came originally from Loch Etive. Our father was James MacIntyre, son of the first settler. The homestead is the original one, added to from the first sod cottage, and it will pass to our nephew when we die. He farms the land and saw your advertisement, so suggested we write you.

'There is plenty of room for your caravan, though we think you would be warmer in the house. There is a well-furnished study for you to work in. If you should take our offer we would be delighted.

'You may like to come to see the place, and us, before deciding, so perhaps you would ring us at the above number if you are interested.

Hoping to hear from you soon,
    Yours sincerely,
        C. Fitzherbert and H. Pomeroy.'

Faith decided to waste no time. It was so ideal she was terrified someone would put the old ladies off it if she didn't get going. Some member of the family might suggest they did it themselves to save money. Though it seemed as if the nephew approved. She dialled the exchange, got the number.

Mrs Pomeroy answered. 'Oh, you *are* a girl. Oh, we're

31

so pleased about that. Do forgive us that we started our letter "Dear Meredith Charteris", but although we know it can be a girl's name, we've known only men called that till now and we're so anxious to get this venture off the ground, we didn't want a man offended because we called him "Miss." So you didn't mind, did you, dear? You sound so nice and young, it will be lovely for Chassie and myself to have someone your age in the house. We don't want to get set in our ways. I remember so many old people when I was young who looked as if they'd never known what it was to giggle in their lives. Of course in those days, with guipure lace fronts to their frocks and piled-up hair with combs, and black velvet bands round their throats, and combinations and camisoles, they seemed older, if you know what I mean!'

Faith felt dazed but managed to say yes, she knew what they meant, and it was different now and of course she didn't mind being called 'Dear Meredith Charteris' and would they——

Mrs Pomeroy anticipated, 'Would we like you to call as soon as possible? Yes, dear, we would. As you've a motel address, perhaps you're not local, so bring your caravan out with you tomorrow, so we can get started as soon as possible. Chassie and I have been living on borrowed time some years now and I'm afraid we've left it a bit late already. We always say we never can tell, we could wake up any morning now in another world and we'd never forgive ourselves if that happened, with the history not written. It would be a lifelong regret. I said to Gareth I must make a New Year resolution nine months ahead of time, so he said for goodness' sake answer this ad. and get cracking, that it was the chance of a lifetime and whatever happened not to put this man off by ear-bashing him on the phone. So I must keep this short or he'll think I put you off by doing what he said I mustn't. What time can you come?' Faith felt as breathless as Mrs Pomeroy ought to be but wasn't. How fortunate they were taking it for granted she would take the position. 'Yes, I'll come tomorrow morning. I have a map. I'll probably be with you about ten.'

They gave her instructions that made her realise joyfully that she'd be very near her target. She almost yelped when they said turn off at Goblin Headland signpost, to take the third turning on the left, after she went under the viaduct. 'Make sure it's the third. It has a coloured stone gateway. The fourth road leads to Lilac Bend and Goblin Head itself. Oh, it will be lovely to have you! We miss the young folk. Our town house is in Oamaru, very near our daughters' homes, and we miss the grandchildren. But we let it when we came out here to keep house for our nephew. We'd better warn you we'll talk your head off!'

Faith managed to say, 'Well, that's the best way of getting information. It's dreadful if you arrive at a place to collect gen and find everyone reserved. It's like trying to get blood out of a stone.'

'Well, you won't find us like that,' said Mrs Pomeroy happily. Faith was sure of that. If *they* lived just two homesteads away from Goblin Head, she was practically sure to meet her father, and to hear all about him.

It was a glorious morning as she crested the motorway. Below her lay limitless shimmering waters, edged by Blueskin Bay. Beyond it were faint and far headlands, one of which would be where her father dwelt. And she would be near, near! She came to the signpost again. No hint of Maori name, though. It must be just the name of the local Post Office. With a singing in her pulses, she turned off, felt metal instead of tarseal under her wheels, dipped under the viaduct, crossed a humpy-backed limestone bridge that surely went back to pioneer days, and began counting turnings.

She saw the third, and the name *Puketaipo* ... so it was the name of the homestead, not the postal district. She went over cattle-stops and swept into the property through an avenue of lombardy poplars so bright that the sun turned them to liquid gold. The fields each side looked more like English parklands than grazing paddocks, though there were Border Leicester ewes in them. They had small copses in the corners, silver birches, cedars, larches, and where the poplars ended, English beeches and oaks spread out, magnificent in their autumn colouring.

Hawthorn hedges showed red haws and rowan berries were vying with the russet of their foliage to make their trees the brightest and best of the trees of the fall.

There were more hedges than wire fences, and they were beautifully trimmed, by machine no doubt, but still reminiscent of a day when life was leisurely and labour cheap. Faith couldn't see a single hay-shed, only haystacks. What a paradise this would be for a painter. They must believe in keeping up the traditions of the past here. She supposed the nephew was elderly too, perhaps resistant to change.

She turned a bend and saw hens outside their fowl-houses on free range. Good, no battery cages here. She was used to noticing these things, from her long training with Stephen.

She drove over more cattle-stops into a garden of yesteryear where, as Goldsmith had said, 'long-departing summer still delayed.'

The homestead was beautifully preserved; built in North Otago limestone, it was whitewashed, had dormer windows and odd gables here and there, in a harmoniously haphazard fashion, and these were outlined in black. A little porch over a side-door was painted green and the fluffy heads of seeded honeysuckle clung to it. Great rambler roses grew against the walls, still in profuse bloom, and she was sure they would bear the names of long-ago strains. Creepers clung lovingly, gnarled wistaria held up arches that would possibly have collapsed long ago otherwise, and nerines in tangerine, gold-dusted, marched in ranks either side of a path of smooth shore-boulders, to the front verandah. The drive branched one

34

way to the front of the house, but also to the back, which would be more suitable for a caravan.

She drove on to a wide area of gravel, but in front of the back door was a courtyard of brick done in herring-bone pattern. The back door flew open and out came two eager figures who looked much younger and more fashionable than she'd expected. As she got out of the car and approached them she realised they were indeed probably in their eighties, but could have passed for seventy.

They held out their hands, their eyes sparkled; both had snowy-white puffs of hair, beautifully styled, but one, Mrs Pomeroy, she found out later, had soft brown eyes and Mrs Fitzherbert had clear blue ones.

She couldn't, at that moment, distinguish who said what.

'How lovely that you're a girl ... and such a pretty one too!' (Faith wondered why that was important!)

'*And* such a gifted one. Dear, you really are an answer to prayer—providential. We aren't procrastinators usually, but we just didn't know where to start. So much material and we can't type. And dear Gareth told us he was so sick and tired of us twittering about it every time we dusted the family treasures that he'd willingly pay Mr Meredith Charteris's wages himself to stop us saying: "We should do something about these records before it's too late." Such a dear boy, and such a shame he's never married. Some woman missed a jewel, and some unborn children a marvellous father.'

Faith grinned to herself. She'd been right. This Gareth could be in his sixties and contrary to his aunt's belief was probably very happy in his bachelor state.

They were certainly wonderful housekeepers for their age. The house positively shone, though that *kauri* stair-rail was gleaming from generations of little hands running down it. A patina, not a polish. She loved it at sight and would have liked to have wandered at will, but they must get down to tintacks.

The old ladies were surprisingly businesslike. They said they knew wages were high but they'd like to pay her standard rates plus something to compensate her for living so far from city amenities. That they had a nest-egg they'd like to use for this. They said it anxiously, eager to clinch matters.

Faith said, 'I'd like to tell you something. I'm not dependent upon this. It's just a project that appeals to me. In surroundings like this it would seem like a holiday. You see, the author I was secretary to was my father and——'

Mrs Pomeroy interrupted, 'Not Stephen Charteris? Yes? Oh, we love his books, so does our nephew. We have them all ... look, on the far side of the fireplace. How grieved we were to read of his death. My dear, how sad for you. He's a loss to the world. In the main, these days, you either get very tame books, which we can't stand, or books that are morbid and depressing and ... what is the word I want Chassie?'

'Ugly, I should think. Some words used in books these days are a prostitution of language, and language can be so beautiful. Your father's books are strong meat, yet never distasteful. We love his characters, his settings, the stories themselves. Oh, dear, I'm afraid Hope and I will trespass on your good nature and simply pepper you with questions about him.'

Faith regained control of the conversation. 'So you see, I'm not yet dependent upon my earnings. Dad's royalties ought to continue for some time. I have some work he left me. His autobiography, in fact, which he prepared but told me by a letter he left to wait some time before publishing it.' She hesitated.

The two white heads nodded. 'That's understandable. He would have a personal reason. You don't have to explain it, dear, go on.'

'So I'd like a position like this, for a few weeks' duration, and I could look on it as almost a holiday. So I'll accept just a minimal wage over and above my keep.'

Surprisingly they were quiet considering that, then looked at each other and nodded. Then Chassie said, 'We've learned, in our very long life, to distinguish sincerity. You have it. We won't insist on the high wage, but to compensate, you must take all the time off you want.'

Faith smiled at them, her grey eyes lighting up. Chassie said, 'My goodness, you *do* remind me of someone. I wonder who. Oh, I suppose I've seen so many pictures of your father on his dust-jackets, that'll be it.'

Faith said, with a truth they'd never guess at, 'Yes, I'm told I greatly resemble my father.' She added, 'I'd better tell you I'm never called Meredith. I just thought it sounded more businesslike. I'm called by a rather old-fashioned name, my second name, Faith. Would you use it?'

The effect was rather startling. The brown eyes met the blue, and both pairs misted over. They smiled, a little tremulously. Then Chassie said, 'It will mean a lot to us. We had a dear older sister. We were the twins. She was Faith. That was why our parents, rather sentimentally in the way of those days, called us Hope and Charity.'

Faith said swiftly, 'If it will be too poignant, I'd be very content to be Meredith.'

They shook their heads. 'No, she died so long ago there isn't any sadness left. We'll love to hear that name in this household again. It will evoke very dear memories.'

Hope said, rising, 'We'll have some tea. I hope you've a good appetite. We love preparing meals. We won't show you to your room yet.' She glanced quickly at Chassie, who nodded, and said, 'Yes, Hope, she must have Faith's room. It's more old-fashioned than the guest-room, but we think you'll like it.'

Faith was struck by a sudden thought. Could this long-ago Faith, of such dear memory to these two, be the Faith her father had wanted her named for? It was quite feasible. It seemed as if there were just two houses beyond this. Lilac Bend and Goblin Head, or Hill, which ever they called it, were on the road she'd turned off to come to *Puketaipo*.

Hope added, 'Faith and her husband died in 1918.'

Faith's mind totted that up. Then she couldn't be named for her. Perhaps it was sheer coincidence, or else Faith was a common name in those days, and it might have been a family name of the Morlands. No doubt she'd find out in time. These chatterboxes would reveal district history as well as the history of the MacIntyres.

She found the bachelor nephew was away for a few days. He was attending sales at the Addington Market in Christchurch and taking delivery of a new car in Oamaru on the way home.

Chassie said, 'He'll be surprised to find you settled in. He pointed out the advertisement to us and said if we were lucky enough to get you, we were on no account to let you take up residence till he got home—thinking you were a man, of course. He probably thought we'd be murdered in our beds and the silver stolen. What a surprise he'll get!'

Faith thought it would probably be a shock. A crabbed old bachelor mightn't want another female invading his home.

Hope giggled. 'Just as well he's away. We've got a little boy coming down from Oamaru, the son of my daughter's neighbour. My daughter was to have him when his mother had her baby, but she's slipped a disc, so we said send him down here. His father's bringing him.'

'Does your nephew not like children?'

'Oh, yes, and very good with them, but he thinks we're past it. Says we've got to stop having tinies here sooner or later. But in the country it's not like the town. They're not having to be watched all the time for traffic.'

Faith resolved her opinion. In the country there were creeks and ponds, farm tractors and all sorts of hazards. But it would be nothing to do with her.

In which she was wrong. Two days later she knew it.

Benjie was a white-headed angel, in looks, with a loving nature, and proved adaptable, but he had also, unfortunately, a rare penchant for getting into mischief.

Today she was looking after him because someone on the other side of the main road had rung up to ask Hope and Chassie to visit her for the afternoon as an old school friend of theirs was staying.

'We dare not take Benjie,' said Chassie. 'They're house-proud. It's a new ranch-style house with never as much as a scratch on any surface. We'd be frustrating Benjie all the time. Take an afternoon off, dear child, and give yourself a break from wading through all those old diaries.'

Entertaining Benjie was a full-time task. To her immense surprise, after cheerfully waving off the old ladies in their car, he sat down and howled non-stop for twenty minutes. Faith had walked him, still wailing inconsolably, all over the rock-shore, pointing out crabs and sea-anemones, cockabullies swimming in the stream the ducks frequented, rescued him from an irate gander who hadn't liked the way Benjie chased his wife, and came to the conclusion that short of being gagged, Benjie would still be performing when Hope and Chassie arrived home.

At that desperate moment Faith caught her foot in a loop of wire and pitched neatly, face first, into a gorse-hedge. Benjie stopped crying in mid-yell to roar unfeelingly with laughter. Faith extricated herself gingerly, wiped blood from the scratches on her face, pulled dry prickles out of her hair and decided it was well worth it.

Thereafter Faith began to enjoy herself. She took him sliding down a half-eaten haystack which improved neither her, Benjie's, nor the haystack's appearance; gave him swings on a tyre suspended from an enormous gum-tree till her shoulders ached, played chasing all through the orchard, gathered the eggs two hours ahead of time ... he'd only dropped four ... one of them clean down Faith's blue slacks; then they gathered two bucketsful of windfall apples and pears.

It was a pity that, as they returned to the house, Benjie had fallen clean over the orchard gate he reached ahead of Faith, right into a foul and muddy pool on the other side. Howls broke out again, his lint-white hair looked as if it had been dipped in tar, his pale blue jersey and long pants to match were caked almost solid. Faith snatched him up and let the buckets go.

She dared not use the bath. The laundry, a modernised small one, opened off the kitchen and held a stainless steel tub beside the washing-machine. She turned on the taps.

Faith swung the bawling Benjie on her hip, looked desperately round for something to wipe off the worst, saw nothing, and, deciding detergents would be too strong for that fair skin, seized some soap flakes and shook the packet so vigorously that the entire contents shot into the warm water. By the time she deposited Benjie in, clothes and all, he practically disappeared from sight in a huge mushroom of suds.

Faith plunged her hands beneath the froth and began peeling his clothes off. She distractedly wiped away a strand of hair that had fallen over her face, leaving a huge streak of green slime across it, and her scratches began to sting. She said imploringly, 'Look, darling, just stop yelling. I'm not killing you, just trying to get you clean!'

Miraculously, Benjie stopped shrieking and into the silence a voice behind her said, 'Who in the world are you?'

She whipped round to see a man in the doorway, young, bulky, broad, tawny. He wore a scowl. Anger? Or just overhanging brows?

Before she could speak he spoke again. 'Don't tell me that you're Mrs Meredith Charteris? And that you've brought a whole family in that caravan? I certainly made a bluey when I pointed out that ad. Look at the place!' He cast a look round the indescribable mess and added: 'I expect you were the one who left those buckets right in the drive. I collected them. It's not improved my brand-new Valiant one bit. Or my temper.'

At the moment the cause of it, peering out of mud and foam, cried joyfully, 'Gareth ... Gareth ... Will you gimme a ride in your new car? I'll soon be clean enough!'

The brows came down even more and the eyes peered from under them like windows below a thatched roof, trying to relate this bodyless head to someone who knew him. 'Good lord, it's Benjie! Heaven help us ... then who are *you*?'

Faith knew she looked a ticket and it made her mad. She hadn't much hope of looking icily dignified, so she said tartly, 'I'm not *Mrs* Meredith Charteris. There isn't one. I *am* Meredith Charteris. Even your aunts knew it might be a woman. It's a woman's name as well as a man's, like other names ... Jocelyn, Hilary, Evelyn, Beverley. There's no sex discrimination there!'

Benjie took the chance of this diversion to scoop with both hands at these lovely suds and gave a terrific puff at them. They descended on the washing-machine, the drier, the deep-freeze, and Faith, to say nothing of the floor.

'Benjie!' said the newcomer in a tone of ultimate authority, 'that's enough of that. Let me talk to Meredith Charteris without interruption.'

'She's not Merediff,' offered Benjie. 'She's Faiff. That's what Aunt Chassie and Aunt Hope call her. It's easier to say.'

'Faith!' said Gareth. 'Tell me, did they know your name was Faith before they engaged you?'

'Well, yes. I told them when they answered my phone-call.'

'No wonder they engaged you. Faith, Hope and Charity again! Good lord!'

She said icily, 'They engaged me to do a job, not on my name. My qualifications are first-class. I merely consented to look after Benjie because they were visiting someone houseproud.'

He surveyed the child. 'Well, for sure they had something there. Pity they hadn't engaged a secretary who knew how to manage children. You've certainly let him make a mess of himself, haven't you?'

'He needed no permission,' said Faith savagely, and thought it sounded childish, pushing the blame on a four-year-old. It made her madder than ever, so she added, 'And Mr MacIntyre, instead of making criticisms, perhaps you'd help by going upstairs to Benjie's room to get some clean clothes for him. Oh, there's some on the rack in the kitchen.'

He made a face. 'Right, but why didn't you arm yourself with a change before you put him in the tub? You didn't know I was going to appear on the scene.'

She lost all patience. 'Ask yourself why! It would have been criminal to track all this mud over those pastel-coloured carpets. Benjie sprayed me from head to foot too.'

He grinned. 'I get you. And by the way, I'm not a MacIntyre. I'm Gareth Morgan.'

As he said it, Benjie gave a banshee wail because he'd rubbed soap in his eye, so Faith couldn't hear correctly. She said, whitening, 'Did you say Morland? Are you——'

Fortunately, he cut in. 'No, not Morland, Morgan.'

Faith gave a sigh of relief she couldn't repress which made him look at her curiously. 'But Morland is my stepfather's name. We often get confused. Perhaps you aren't *au fait* with the situation here. You soon will be if you're attempting the family history. I work this end of the estate, my stepfather works the other—at Lilac Bend, the other house. He and my mother are still in Canada visiting relations of hers. Chass and Hope are my stepfather's aunts. Benjie, stop bawling.'

He took out his handkerchief, gently wiped Benjie's eyes. 'Now stay still. I'll get the clothes, Miss Charteris.'

He disappeared. Faith felt stunned. Hope and Chassie were not *neighbours* of her father's. They were his aunts, so her own great-aunts. Then this Gareth was her step-brother! If only she'd dipped into the more recent family anecdotes, she'd have found that out. It wasn't a Morland estate, it was a MacIntyre one. What a complication! Now, if she ever made herself known as Philippa's god-daughter, they'd wonder why she hadn't said so at first.

She was on the estate, but her father was still thousands of miles away. She might be finished this task by the time he got back. No other house was visible from here. Oh, if only she'd realised this house was part of it! Her father must be the son of Hope and Chassie's sister. She'd not heard of her yet. Oh, if only the name on that swinging wooden shingle at the cattle-stops had said Goblin Hill, she'd have known, and would have turned back and rung them to make some excuse. She felt she'd wormed her way in under false pretences. It was one thing to take a position at a neighbour's, quite another to invade their home.

She went on madly wiping. His hair was now reasonably clean. She seized a towel, spread it on the laundry table and lifted him out, and turned the cold tap on full so it would swish the suds down the drain. He was standing there, stark naked, foam dripping off him, when Gareth Morgan arrived back with a pile of clothes, two towels and a face-cloth.

He seemed to have mellowed, because he liked the idea of clean warm water being run in the tub to rinse Benjie. He helped her, making a more thorough job of Benjie's hair. 'That pool's been by the gate for weeks. It's really stagnant. It reeks. So do you.'

Faith flushed. 'Well, if you care to keep him out of mischief a few moments longer I'll kick off my shoes and dash up to the bathroom myself.'

He noticed the flush and said dryly, 'It was meant as a joke, so you don't have to behave like those daft females on the commercials when they're told they've got bad breath. I'm a farmer, after all. I fell in a cow-platter just last week. You'd better develop a sense of humour if you're to be here any length of time.'

'My sense of humour's never been in question before,' she retorted, kicked off her shoes and marched upstairs.

'It's all right, Gareth,' she heard Benjie say consolingly as she went. 'It's me she's mad at.'

She was determined to appear before him impeccably clad. She donned a gun-metal grey dress with white collar and cuffs trimmed with black saddle-stitching, plain court shoes in black, brushed her short brown hair till it shone, applied make-up sparingly but expertly, and her only touch of colour was a cherry-coloured bow at her brown throat.

He whistled as she entered the kitchen where he was buttering scones. 'Now I can believe you were once secretary to an author.'

Faith said, 'Your aunts——'

'My great-aunts,' he corrected her.

She sighed. 'Your great-aunts asked was it possible I'd been secretary to Stephen Charteris. It was. He was also my father. I assure you I do have experience in typing, editing, sifting, filing.'

He said, 'You'd have to be that if you were a Charteris. His accuracy is amazing. Perhaps you were responsible for that.'

'For some of it,' she admitted. 'He taught me to be that way.' This seemed better. She wouldn't want to antagonise her father's stepson right off.

Gareth Morgan made a swoop at Benjie. 'You'll sit up to the table with that, young man. No going round with a jammy scone wiping it on chairs and sofas. Up you come, and there's your milk.' He was managing Benjie a lot better than she had.

He poured the tea. Perhaps he thought her a fool when it came to housewifely virtues. She'd show him.

He bit into a scone and gave her the opportunity. 'My word, these are good! Fresh too, much nicer than thawed from the freezer. Other things freeze well, but I do like scones fresh. Did they make them before they went out?'

'No, I made them after lunch.'

'Good show!' He was mellowing.

Faith said, 'Thus far I've dealt only with pioneer records—in fact pre-pioneer days. I was looking up the descent of the MacIntyres. I found they possessed land in Kintyre, and around Loch Etive. No wonder, seeing it's a sea-loch, they settled here. I'm still researching forebears in Scotland. I hadn't realised this was part of the Goblin Hill estate. There was a Maori name down at the gate.'

He grinned. 'Same thing. *Puketaipo*. *Puke* is hill, *Taipo* is goblin. This is the Goblin Hill homestead itself.'

She blinked. 'Oh, I've always known *Puke* means hill, but I thought *Tipua* was goblin.'

'It is, but it has other meanings too. It can also mean foreigner and devil, but our goblin is a kindly one.'

She said cautiously, 'I might sound prying, but I'm writing the history. How come it's run by a Morland, not a MacIntyre?'

'Well, Dad, my stepfather, is the only male left in the family, of MacIntyre descent. He's the son of Prudence MacIntyre and Robert Morland. Hope and Chassie had daughters, and they in turn have no sons. Prudence and Robert are retired in Oamaru now, but they lived here when my mother married Julian Morland and built them a house called Lilac Bend further up Goblin Head. You can't see it from here. There's a married couple's house up there too. I've got two sisters. I'm to farm the land when Dad retires because he has no children of his own, but that time's a long way off. He's no age. I've promised to call my son, if I have one, MacIntyre as a second name. That's why I'm glad the family history is to be written at last, because the written word is imperishable. A book lasts. So much of today's media has only a passing hour and vanishes from the screen. But things that are written go into the Archives of the Alexander Turnbull Library in Wellington and are preserved for always.'

A strange feeling swept over Faith. 'Because my stepfather has no children of his own.' But he has, he has! He has a daughter. Nevertheless, those might be words she would never dare to utter.

Benjie had finished. Faith wiped his fingers, allowed him to get down. He began playing with dominoes on the floor.

Suddenly Gareth Morgan looked her straight in the eye. 'I'm very glad you prefer to be called Faith rather than Meredith.'

She looked a little startled. 'Because you've only known it as a man's name?'

'No. Look, I think I should tell you. I suppose you, like most people, watch *The Pengarths of the Cove*?'

He didn't hear her catch her breath because she checked it as soon as it began. She nodded.

'Then you'll know Philippa Meredith's acting, and possibly that though she's been in England over twenty-five years, she was originally a New Zealander?'

She nodded.

'She's a great actress—I hand her that. But she was my stepfather's first wife and treated him very cruelly. Dad's one of the very best. It went deep. She left him and New Zealand because she wanted a career. She ought never to have married a farmer. The years after she left him must have been very lonely for him. Then he and my mother married. My own father had been a farmer, but not a hard-working one like Julian Morland. Mother did all the sacrificing for us. My father lost the farm through drink, horses, the lot. Then he died.

'Life began again for Mother when she married Julian Morland. She had a purpose in life. That was making up to him for all the loneliness he'd known, for all he'd suffered at the hands of that Philippa Meredith. But, on viewing figures, that series is the most popular TV programme of any. Isn't that so?'

Faith nodded. Her lips felt too stiff to frame words.

'Can you imagine what it's like? Twice a week for five years Dad's beautiful first wife has flaunted herself on our screen! She comes right into our living-room. When it first started my sisters were home. Everyone was talking about this new series. It's magnificent acting. Mother and Dad wouldn't let it seem to matter. I got the girls together, had a discussion and then we told them we thought it could be painful to both, and if so, the girls were willing to forgo it too.

'I think Mother's acting and Dad's far surpassed anything Philippa Meredith has ever portrayed. You've no idea how genuine they sounded. Dad said she was just something that happened to him so long ago it was just like a dream in the night. Mother said she felt so secure in their happiness and in Dad's love that nothing could disturb it. That on the screen Philippa Meredith meant nothing to her. I remember my sisters were so thrilled. They felt this real-life romance outdid anything they'd ever seen on television.

'I'm afraid I wasn't so impressed. I'd seen Mother act before when my own father was alive and she'd been desperately worried—sometimes afraid—bitterly disillusioned. Yet before us she was mostly so gay, so philosophical.

'I didn't even dare shun the programme. Mother would have guessed how I hated Philippa Meredith's charm and vitality if I had. But I skipped it whenever a good excuse presented itself. *And now she's dead*. It's over. When I heard the announcement on TV and read the headlines, I was *glad*. I wanted my mother to have some life without that woman from her husband's past overshadowing her.'

Faith felt as if someone had taken her heart in a giant grip and squeezed it. She had found her mother only when her span of life was ebbing fast. Those days had been so fleeting, so precious. Now this man was glad she was dead. But, even if it burned her like acid, she could understand his feelings.

He continued, 'I believe that, at her own wish, they're writing her out, that she portrays her own death on the screen. I've no doubt it will be done superbly. They'll wring every last drop of anguish out of that incident. I think it's going to be hell for Mother and Dad.' He looked up and surprised tears in the wide grey eyes across the table from him. 'Oh, sorry, I've gone on too much. One does sometimes. And all I wanted to do was impress upon you that I'd rather they didn't even know your first name was Meredith. She's gone, and as soon as she's written out, the better. I'm thankful that not only a chapter of life is closed, but the whole book.'

Maybe Faith had, after all, inherited a little of her mother's talent, because she gave nothing away. Perhaps Benjie helped, because he had to be watched, because he interrupted them in their subsequent conversation. She learned that Gareth's parents were beginning to get a little tired of jaunting about the world and he wouldn't be surprised any time to hear they were on their way back.

She was pretty sure he hadn't been told that his brave little mother had sought Philippa Meredith out and taken Julian to see her, too.

She also realised that what he'd told her had put paid to her own dreams of revealing herself. She would never be a living reminder of an unhappy past for two people of the calibre of Leonie and Julian Morland.

CHAPTER THREE

THE situation was eased considerably when the aunts got home. It was inevitable they should say: 'Have you been a good boy, Benjie?'

Benjie said stoutly, 'I've been a very good boy. I picked up all the apples and pears and got all the eggs out of the nests.' But he cast an anxious look at Faith.

She said at once, lightly, 'And since then Benjie and I have both washed and changed ready for dinner. He helped me scrub the potatoes—we're having jacket potatoes with the cold duck—and scraped the radishes. That's a job I don't like doing. So the salad's all ready.'

She was most relieved that this nephew of theirs didn't add sarcastically that the pears and apples were now mush on his chariot wheels, that his new Valiant was wearing a scratch on its right front wing. She must be thankful for that.

The aunts twittered on happily about their afternoon out, repeating to Gareth the trivial gossip of the district, so Faith's preoccupation went unremarked. She was thinking that the sooner she finished here the better and she could leave without any of them the wiser. Nevertheless, she knew a relief that she wasn't likely to complete it till Julian and Leonie Morland arrived home, so she would have some memories, at least, of her father.

She came up from her reverie to hear Hope say, 'These ducks are delicious cold, but the way Faith served them last night was out of this world.'

The brows twitched. 'Good heavens, Aunt Hope, don't tell me she cooked last night's dinner too? I thought she was here as an amanuensis, not a home-help!'

He sounded more exasperated than amused. Faith felt her hackles rising. She said tartly, 'Mr Morgan, I cooked the dinner last night *after* seven hours at my desk. But today I had an idea pioneer research and Benjie just wouldn't mix.'

He said calmly, 'You made your point there ... at the very moment we met, and visually, not verbally. It's not you I'm taking to task, it's Aunt Chass and Aunt Hope. They'll use you exactly as they want to use you. True products of a more leisurely age, they are. Oh, they may have just scraped into the Victorian era by the skin of their teeth, but the way they go on, they might just as well have been born in its heyday, instead of its last decade. The way my beloved aunts conduct their lives one would think they'd never heard of unions, Women's Lib, inflation, and the permissive age!'

Benjie said plaintively, 'I dunno what Gareth's talking about.'

'Neither does anyone else,' said Charity Fitzherbert.

'Oh, *I* do,' said Faith, 'but he'd better know *I'm* not one who despises Victorian ways. There's a load of rubbish talked about lives as lived then and it's overdone. It's a little too close to the present time, that's all. Given another couple of generations, and it could seem as glamorous as the eighteenth century!'

She was beginning to notice Gareth Morgan had a rather infuriating drawl at times. It sounded now. 'Oh, I assure you, Miss Charteris, that at least in that, we're on the same wavelength. I admire the Victorians. *I* don't see their women as meek and submissive and as oppressed as the historians would have us believe.'

Faith decided to switch. 'No? ... then will you tell me why all that suffragette business was necessary? Overseas, anyway. I know we had the vote here for women long before the turn of the century.'

'Oh, I admit women had a raw deal legally then, so it was right to fight for it. I just mean that all the Victorian women I've heard tell of, in the stories that have been handed down from generation to generation, got more of their own way than they get credit for now. They had prettier ways of getting it, that's all. Like Hope and Charity here ... look at them ... like Dresden china shepherdesses, all womanly grace, and as tough as steel. We all dance to their piping, and, blow me down, find ourselves liking to do it. We play host to everyone who tells a good tale, manage the farm according to pioneer custom in many things, spruce up for the evening meal ... oh, yes, Goblin Hill is run according to the wishes of Hope and Charity. Be warned, Miss Charteris. You've already been roped in as cook to the household, nanny to Benjie, and you'll be lucky if you ever get round to writing the history at all.

'I might just prove you wrong. It's not for me working at my typewriter when the mood takes me. I observe very strict rules, and my break today will be made up at the weekend when, according to the gospel of the forty-hour week, that's my off-time.'

Hope and Chassie were laughing girlishly at all this, regarding their nephew-by-marriage with a fond eye. 'But you do appreciate the orange glazing on the ducklings, don't you, Gareth?' continued Hope as if there'd been no disgression. 'She didn't overdo it, but coated it perfectly. It had just a hint of lemon rind in it, gives it a tang. There was some over, so I had it on my icecream too, last night. And she makes her bed beautifully, just like Mother taught us. I never have to sneak in and smooth out the wrinkles like I had to when we had that Sylvia creature staying here to help in the house. And you'd never know she'd been in the bathroom ... no splashes on the floor. Even the way she listens encourages us to talk.'

Gareth muttered, 'As if that was necessary!' but Chassie took up the cudgels on her twin's behalf. 'We don't mean just chatterboxing, Gareth, we mean she somehow inspires us to remember everything we ever heard from Mother and Father. We could have got someone who'd have put us out of our stride by looking, if not saying, we'd already told her more than enough anecdotes. I know we'll bog her down. But she seems to be able to select. And we might have got someone who'd expect to be waited upon. Some journalists are like that, so other-worldly you could shake them. Not practical at all. I remember how our mother used to parody the thirteenth chapter of Corinthians. ... "Though I speak with the tongues of men and of angels and have not gumption, I am become as sounding brass, or a tinkling cymbal. I may have all the gifts of art, music, and letters, and all the graces that society demands, but if I have not gumption, I am a misfit." Faith here is just full of gumption. What do you want, dear?'

'My notebook. Oh, the telephone pad will do. That's a thumbnail sketch of your mother's personality. It makes her come before me even more vividly than her photograph. Another dimension. What fun she must have been! Olivia MacIntyre is now as real to me as you two are.'

As Faith scribbled, then laid the pad beside her plate, she caught a gleam of something in Gareth Morgan's eyes. Something not quite so hostile.

A pity then that Chassie and Hope continued to lay it on with a trowel. Faith, they informed Gareth, wasn't one who believed in burning the midnight oil and taking till mid-morning to get over it. She liked to rise early, to get a good start. She had insisted on setting up her caravan as a study, so the house wouldn't be cluttered with old photos, letters, diaries, accounts. 'She finds the prices so fascinating, and some of the items—the tallow, the yards of wicks for the candles, the button-boots, the face-veils. She's so careful to check everything. She already has a list a yard long of things she must verify at Dunedin public library and the Early Settlers Museum. And to find out that, despite all that knowledge at her fingertips, she liked housework too, was just marvellous.'

Faith felt like screaming. She sounded such a paragon, and she knew she was far from that. That as a child she'd been as lazy as the next one, but Lucy, in her gentle way, had been a disciplinarian, insisting that she learned how to cope with everyday tasks, 'Then you'll be their master, Faith, they'll never get on top of you. Subdue the tendency to leave the jobs you hate. Get them done first and the others will come easily.'

Now, Faith quenched her desire to recount all the things she didn't excel at, and said instead, lightly, 'You sound as if you're trying to sell me, Mrs Pomeroy and Mrs Fitzherbert.'

'Oh, they *are* trying to do just that,' said Gareth, accepting his portion of Norwegian trifle topped with cream, and mulberries, from her. 'They always do.'

She looked puzzled. '*Always* do? What do you mean? I've just come.'

He grinned shamelessly. 'Always try to sell me every unattached female who dawns on the Goblin Hill horizon. It doesn't worry me, I see through it. It's an occupational hazard. Every bachelor over thirty years suffers from it.'

Faith felt as if the fury that threatened to overwhelm her must be visible, but she managed a creditable chuckle as if she too found it absurd. Words spilled out of her before she had time to realise it was no longer true.

'What a good thing then that *I'm* not heart-whole and fancy-free. You're in no danger from me, Mr Morgan, so relax. I see what you mean about the Victorians. Your aunts feel you're wasting your sweetness on the desert air. Isn't it odd how things change? One time it was the role of the single girls to try to assert that marriage wasn't the be-all and end-all of existence, that some of them preferred a career. It's time you men started a counter-movement. You could carry banners proclaiming: "Down with matchmaking mothers and aunts. We don't all want matrimony. We're single-minded." I hope it'll come to pass for poor oppressed males.'

The aunts were dabbing their eyes with lace-bordered handkerchiefs. 'Oh, won't Prudence enjoy Faith?' said

Chassie. 'Do you remember how she used to go on just like this? Our father, even, couldn't down her, and he was a great one for an argument. He was always wondering aloud where he got her from. Always said it was a pity she had to be born in New Zealand. That if her grandfather hadn't emigrated, she would have made an indomitable suffragette.'

Faith wanted to know more. They were talking of her very own grandmother. 'But *she* didn't hold out for a career?' she asked.

They laughed. 'She fell for Robert Morland—head over heels. No half-measures there. Robert is a masterful sort—so right for Prudence.'

Faith said, with hope, 'Do they come out here often?'

Gareth answered that. 'Sure thing. Robert Morland is hale and hearty for his age. He ran the estate for years. I don't know how we'd get on without him yet in the rush times. You'll like both of them, I'm sure.'

Joy mixed with pain overwhelmed Faith momentarily. How she longed to claim kinship with her own grandparents! How she longed to say to Gareth, 'Not *your* beloved aunts, but mine!'

But she couldn't ever, because it would cause Leonie pain. Leonie who had taken her father's shattered life and fitted the pieces together again. The woman who'd been courageous enough to visit Julian's first wife, but who now, when she knew that sight of her would finally cease to invade their living-room at Goblin Head every week, might know a vast sense of relief and freedom from an unhappy past. Faith mustn't give herself away, or this tawny-browed man would see that she was gone from Puketaipo before her father came home.

Fortunately Benjie caused a diversion. Faith had to swoop to right the bowl of mulberries. 'I'll help you to some more, love. They make an awful mess of the table-cloth!'

She thought Gareth's smile irritatingly magnanimous.

'Well, I'll forgive you neglecting the family chronicles for a dessert like this.'

She knew a small satisfaction at putting him in the wrong. 'I didn't make it. Your aunts did before they went out.'

Hope said quickly, 'But she told us how. I asked had she any recipes up her sleeve, for a change for us. It's so simple, just a whip of eggs and gelatine and sugar, with raspberry jam spread under the cream.'

Benjie said, 'I've had a bath, so can I have twice as long a story-time? Gareth, will you tuck me in and tell me about being wrecked on the Sumner Bar the time you and Uncle Julian took the launch to Christchurch and the lifeboat had to put out?'

Gareth said, 'Sure. I'll dodge drying the dishes that way.' He sighed. 'I suppose it's the little room off mine?' He bent a stern look on his aunts. 'I knew it. *You* get the credit for the hospitality. *I* get wakened up too early in the mornings. Anyway, if I spin it out that story will keep me out of the way of most of *The Pengarths*.'

Faith flinched. Her mother's serial. *She* wasn't going to miss a moment of it. She hoped Benjie delayed him for all of it.

He didn't. Gareth came down, settled himself in a big wing chair, said, 'He didn't even last out till the wave swamped the boat, which means he'll be into my bed at half-past five tomorrow morning, wanting the rest of it.'

Providentially Hope and Charity hushed him down quite fiercely. 'We don't want to miss any of this. It's just beautiful. And if the phone rings, *you* answer it, Gareth, on the extension in the study!'

He picked up the paper. Faith felt she'd scream if he rustled it, but perhaps he'd been told so often not to, he stuck to one page.

It could hardly have been more poignant. No hint of illness had yet hollowed Philippa's cheeks, or grooved lines of pain about her mouth, but Faith could see how wistfulness had etched her features more sharply. No doubt the aunts would put it down to superb acting, but only Faith, of all her viewers, would know these lines were not learned by rote, but came from Philippa's own experience, from her heart. Mark would have known when he was directing it.

The colour set did it full justice. Phillippa, as Tamar Pengarth, was standing at a window, watching the sun set over the Atlantic. Carlyon Pengarth, her husband, wanting the comfort of his hearthside and pipe, and the window shut excluding draughts, called to her from the doorway of the other room, 'Tamar, Tamar, come in to the hearthfire, woman. Will you never let a sun set over the cove without you watching from yon casement? Your children are in their beds and wanting you to kiss them goodnight. Leave the sunset. What does it matter?'

Tamar turned from the window, the flowing chestnut hair rippling over the laced bodice fashionable then, her green eyes meeting her husband's.

'Oh, Carlyon, husband, have you never guessed through all these years? Never realised that I come here to bid my other child goodnight? I am not just the mother of the two children who lived, Carlyon, but of the little lost one too. And our Wenefrede always seems so near me at sunset-time, when she left us. For when I stand here and gazebeyond the bourne of sea and land into that realm of sky and cloud and colour, I believe in life eternal. I believe that someday God will give me back the lost years. The years of her childhood I did not see or hear.

'No one save a mother who has borne her child within her for nine long months, who has known the joy of life stirring beneath her heart, and the travail of birth bringing its small face to her sight, can understand the anguish of losing that life before it had time to flower. So, dear one, each night I keep a small tryst with her. I ask: "What new word did you learn today, my darling? What new beauty of that other world dawned upon your sight?" And I say: "Tell me about it someday," and

I am warmed and comforted, Carlyon, and I can come in to my other children and tuck their quilts about them and tell them their stories with no sadness on my brow or grief in my voice. For childhood should be a happy time, and that hour verged close on sleep should be one of peace and joy.'

Faith had no need to feel embarrassed because her lashes were wet, because so were Chassie's and Hope's. She felt a tightness in her midriff as she blinked hastily and hoped she wouldn't react sharply if Gareth twitted them on their sentimentality. But he didn't.

She'd been vaguely aware during this scene that he'd lowered his paper; that he'd watched and listened too. Perhaps he admired the acting though detesting the actress. She was glad the aunts seemed to have no such inhibitions. But then they had the wisdom and experience of age.

She had to control a strong desire to chatter nervously, afraid of comments on Philippa, afraid they'd begin to tell her that she had been their nephew's first wife in a disastrous marriage that hadn't lasted, but apparently even chatterboxes had their reserves. Faith was glad of that. A rollicking comedy followed, good, light relief. Laughter was so cleansing, so healing. When Faith went to bed she slept exhaustedly.

Every morning Faith knew delight in waking up in her long-dead Great-aunt Faith's bedroom, watching the sunlight slant through the chintzy curtains, glint on the old-fashioned gilt-framed pictures, pick out the silver printing on the ancient photograph albums in the fretwork bookcases that the pioneer MacIntyre had made for his eldest granddaughter so long ago. But this morning she woke with a heavy heart, remembering that what Gareth Morgan had revealed of his feelings had put paid to her ever risking telling her father he had a daughter.

She could do nothing about it. She would piece together this family history. Her father would want that, too, not just the aunts. That, at least, would be one way in which she could serve him. If it was to go from the first turning of the sods that had comprised the original cottage walls, to the present day, then he, no doubt, would have stories of his own to add to it. At that thought her heart stirred. What a bitter-sweet time it would be!

But when she left she would have memories of her own to tide over lonelier days. She would have met her grandparents by then too. And she was thankful just to have been privileged to know Goblin Hill.

How strangely strong were the ties of family. Faith remembered a writer friend of her foster-father's, who'd gone to the Isle of Wight. She was a New Zealander, but it was from the Isle that her grandfather, in the eighteen-fifties, had left home, never to return, and this woman had known the strongest, most painful feeling of being torn between two places ... New Zealand, where her family and friends lived, and this lovely sea-girt island, sweet with cuckoo-notes, sculpted with deep chines and fairy-like grottoes, rolling meadows, thatched roofs, where lay her ancestral roots.

Faith now knew a kinship with that woman. She crossed to the latticed windows of the dormer, flung them wide, leaned on the sill. A rose nodded in. Hope had told her the name of it just yesterday—not a flamboyant new one, an old one called Pinkie. It was white, with a flush of pink at its heart. Hollyhocks strove to reach the sill from the bed below, lavender, past its best now, still flung fragrance on the air. Far beyond, that shimmering sea swept bluely to a lilac and gold horizon; on the slopes beyond the garden the sweet, tangy native bush clustered to the cliff edge almost, hiding the paths that led to the shore.

Near at hand virginia creeper was bright where it clung to the old limestone outhouses, sheep baaed faintly from paddocks in the distance, fowls clucked contentedly as they scratched, sparrows kept up a twittering to remind the aunts that the bird-table hadn't been replenished, *tuis* and bellbirds rang out notes of sweetness, and above all rose a lark's song, so highly soaring it wasn't even a speck against the azure.

Her sort of place. Her very own home where she might have grown up, loved and wanted. Only her young mother's foolishness denied her daughter her birthright. That, and the bitterness in a man's heart against the woman who'd so wounded his loved stepfather.

Faith heard voices, footsteps, looked down, saw Gareth Morgan and Benjie approaching the stable-gate. The Peruvian Bronze Valiant was outside the stable. Benjie's voice floated up. 'We didn't ought to have left those buckets there, did we, Gareth? But we were so wet and dirty. But we'll know next time, won't we?'

The scowling stranger of yesterday actually chuckled. 'Are you aiming to repeat it, Benjie? I must warn Miss Charteris.'

'I don't call her that. I can't say Chart-a-wiss. I call her Faiff. Why don't you?'

'Well, it's hardly worth while. She's here for such a short time. Now, Benjie, you can rub that dust off the scratch with this. I sandpapered it down last night. I'll get the paint—good thing I always get a bit of the same shade when I buy a new car. I'll get it done expertly when I'm in Oamaru next, but this'll save the rust settling in.'

'That's what Daddy always does He fumped me when I scratched *his* new car. I expect *you* couldn't very well fump me because you'd have had to fump Faiff too, and that'd never do, would it?'

'I admit I'd have enjoyed thumping her in the first five minutes, but I've got a lovely nature and soon forgave her. I told the aunts we might be a bit late for breakfast. With a bit of luck we might manage it all on our own, Benjie.'

Faith turned swiftly from the window. If she skipped a shower, she'd be finished before they came in. Pity the aunts were so leisurely. She said briskly as she sat down,

'No porridge or bacon-and-egg for me this morning, my dears. Just toast and marmalade. I'm not used to this and at this rate my clothes won't fit me.'

Aunt Hope twittered, 'Oh, and we were so enjoying feeding you up. You know, dear, that sort of breakfast's all right in town, but with country and sea air you'll find an edge on your appetite.'

'Well, it may be country, but my work's still sedentary and I don't need it. I'm going to be flat out today. Yesterday I got all the notes ready for that first chapter. I'll make my morning coffee in the caravan and stay over there.'

Aunt Chassie looked like a disappointed child. 'Oh, we were about to suggest you went out with Gareth and Benjie in the jogger cart. It's such fun. He wants to do a round seeing he's just got back. You've never been over to see the ranch-house or the married couple's house.'

Faith was aware that Gareth and Benjie were now scrubbing up at the basin on the back verandah. 'I'm equally sure he's as busy as I am, and will be grateful to me for not taking that offer. I'd rather explore on foot some time. That's the best way of all. On your own, just rambling.'

'Or wif me,' said Benjie gallantly as he entered. 'I'll show you all the places you can't go to.'

'Such as?' asked Faith.

'The Blow-hole on the cliffs. You've got to hold someone's hand there, because peering down makes you giddy. And you can't climb that blasted tree.'

Faith looked startled. Gareth, coming in, explained, 'It was blasted by lightning and is absolutely rotten. Benjie fell into the middle once and by the time we got him out we were all as black as he was.'

Benjie hurried on, 'And you're not allowed to move any levers on the tractor, or touch the crosscut saw, and you can go in the loft as long as you don't try hanging head down. You can slip. But now I'm big I don't do any of those things.'

Gareth said, 'Surely you're not finished, Miss Charteris? What a breakfast!'

Faith had risen. 'That's enough for my sort of job. And by the way, I'd like no interruptions till I'm called for lunch. And don't be so polite. It's always been my experience that menfolk like breakfast on their own.' She felt rather pleased.

The days passed methodically. Especially when Benjie went back to town. Faith's first rough copy grew into a respectable pile. She thought Gareth approved of her methods. She divided her time into research, taking notes, and typing.

His first look of approval came when he realised that every night she locked the top copy of the rough in a steel cabinet drawer in the caravan and brought the carbon over to old Duncan's study. In case of fire destroying one, she said.

He came in as she was slipping it into a drawer of the old pioneer's desk Chassie had put at her disposal. She explained, 'I was told you never used this desk for the farm accounts, that you always used the one in the window.'

He looked at her. 'You don't need to sound so much on the defensive. Look, I admit I was a bit put out when I found out Meredith Charteris wasn't a man—but if you'd known what a time I'd had with——'

She cut in, 'Oh, spare me the details of your conquests. I'm here to do a job, not to become too involved with family.'

She expected the brows to descend. Instead he laughed. 'Good for you, and serve me right! Sounded insufferable, didn't I? And you are doing a damned good job. You're the only person I've ever known who can keep the aunts from frittering away her time. I love them dearly, but it's a work of art keeping them to the point. I'm lost in wonder, love and praise many a night the way you keep their stories in chronological order. They're so inconsequential, it would drive me up the wall. And the way you so unerringly sift out fact from legend, history from family prejudice is wonderful. And chance of looking over what you've done so far? I've a free night.'

She hesitated. 'Normally I'm like any writer, hate people seeing my work in the unpolished state, but as this is fact, you might pick up the odd mistake here and there. I've far too much stuff, and I'll hate to cull some of it. It's not like in thrillers or novels, if you've too much material you know it will be used in another book in a different way. Yet I feel that it must all go into the rough. Make sense to you?'

'Yes, it does. And as you type your rough, it will preserve, in an unpolished form, even what you have to delete. Nice to have it all for future generations. I'd appreciate seeing what you've done so far. Of course it's not my own family history, but I've lived here so long, and on my own with the aunts for some time now, and they're such good storytellers, I identify with the MacIntyres. I almost feel Scots myself, instead of mainly Welsh.'

Faith nodded. 'It's a great pity there aren't more storytellers of their calibre. My father sought them out all his life. They're so conscious of the past that it seems to be with us still. I feel I know Duncan and Euphemia, his girl-wife. What courage! Perhaps the clan motto served them well. *Per ardua*—through difficulties. They certainly overcame all obstacles. Phemy seemed so gay, so irrepressible. I like to think of Faith as a little girl being the darling of old Duncan's heart. After nothing but sons I supposed he adored his first granddaughter.'

She looked reflective. 'And how sad to think that in the next generation there were no sons. Nice if the name had carried on. Still, you'll incorporate it in your son's name, I hear.'

She looked up to find him staring at her fixedly. For once she felt at a loss with him. He said, the tawny-brown eyes holding hers, 'I thought you said you didn't want to get involved with the family. I think you're in, boots and all.'

She said quickly, 'I'm always like that when I'm on a job. Dad said I used to identify with his characters as much as he did. But when this job is finished I'll be just as involved with the next.'

'And what will that be?'

She wished she'd not got on to this topic. 'I'm not sure.'

'Haven't you any unfinished work of your father's? I'd like to think we got something more from his pen. That shelf over there, of Stephen Charteris's books, could hold a couple more. Didn't he leave any manuscripts behind?'

'Not really. There are two still to be published. But Dad knew his time was short. He finished everything except——'

'Except what?'

She said slowly, 'Except his autobiography. He'd worked on it, at intervals, for years. But now——'

'You mean if you finished it, it wouldn't be an *auto*-biography?

'No. Because it would need very little adding to it. Just a paragraph or two to explain that he'd not lasted long after his Lucy. It was a true love-match, that.'

His look was sympathetic. 'I expect you couldn't face typing it in the first few months after his death. I can understand that. And to do it, living in the home you shared with them, might be too poignant. Would you like to stay on here when you finish ours, and do it? Have you the material in the caravan?'

The kindness of the offer took her by surprise. Then she said, 'It's in safe-deposit in Napier.'

'You could send for it. That way you'd be here when the proofs of this come back from the printers. I mean, seeing we're having a private edition done, it will be quicker than a book that has to be considered and accepted. Why not?'

'It's not as simple as that. Dad left a letter for me. I

could add something—or not—at my discretion.'

'Oh. Well, it must be very personal for him to make such a provisio—so I won't pry further. It's solely over to you. Nothing to do with anyone else.'

Little did he know it was everything to do with him, with his mother, his stepfather. The solicitor had kept this letter till her return from England. In it Stephen had said if she now knew who her parents were, and they were willing, the true story of that time twenty-five years ago could be revealed—the circumstances of her adoption. 'Because I feel that when both Lucy and myself have gone, Philippa may want to claim you as her own. I feel—have always felt—she would have taken you back when she made her way, but would not hurt either Lucy or myself. And your father was a fine man, he may be very happy to know he has a daughter.'

She didn't know how sad and perplexed her face was, remembering.

Gareth tugged at the polo-neck of the big oatmeal-coloured jersey he was wearing. 'Rather hot in here, isn't it? I'll dampen that fire down with a bit of wet dross.' The *manuka* logs cut on the estate were solid and fierce.

He turned round from the hearthrug. 'I thought the delay might have been due to your preferring to do it after you're married.'

She looked a little blank, recovered quickly. 'Oh, there's no date fixed. You may have noticed I'm not wearing a ring.'

'Odd he let you come away down here without one.'

Oh, dear, she must go warily. Pity she'd been stung into saying she wasn't heartwhole and fancy-free. But she'd been so mad with him.

'Well, it was so soon after Dad's death. I wanted to be away by myself for a bit.'

He brushed up the slack he'd spilled. His back was towards her. 'What's his name, and what does he do?'

She knew she mustn't hesitate. 'Glen Tankerville, and he's in the Town Planner's Office.'

He looked surprised as he swung round. 'Fair go? Must be the attraction of opposites. You're the very essence of a country girl.'

Oddly, seeing she'd finished with Glen, she took umbrage. 'I do prefer the country, yes, but it's always happening. Isn't that why we admire the young Euphemia so much? ... brought up in the city of Edinburgh, a silversmith's daughter, reared in the lap of luxury, coming here with Duncan, to finally build in a place reached only by bullock-track? Why should that be so admirable, and a country-loving girl putting up with town life to be despised? Am I to find out, living here, that there's a certain class-consciousness after all? that the sons of pioneer families are rather snooty about their town brethren?' The grey eyes fairly shot sparks.

He rose from his haunches, burst out laughing, took her by the shoulders, gave her a little shake. 'Oh, Faith, you make me laugh! The aunts are right—you're just like Prudence Morland. She's got the same angelic cast of features, but fires up just as readily. It's a daunting combination!'

Faith caught her bottom lip between her teeth. *So she was like her grandmother in features?* Unaware, he rushed on, 'And may I remind you I'm no descendant of fine pioneers! In fact, my own father was a no-gooder. So do acquit me of any snobbery, though I admit you were right to take me up on that. It was a damn silly thing to say. Don't know why I said it. Perhaps it's just that you look so right in this setting. I just can't think of you in the city.' He laughed. 'Good job you're spoken for, girl, or the aunts would weave their webs about the two of us.'

Faith said tartly, 'So it's just as well they know my situation.' She looked reflective, and purposely wicked. 'I'll never forget how relieved you looked when you found that out, Mr Morgan, you poor thing. What a hunted life you must have had!' She added, 'But you feel less scared of me now, don't you? Is that why you unbent enough to call me Faith just now?'

'Probably. I just didn't think about it.'

'Look, Mr Morgan, I must get on. I've so much stuff to look through. I'd hate to miss something vital. Here's the rough for you to take through to the living-room.'

'Oh, I'm staying here to read it. Can't concentrate with television on, and the aunts are going to be glued to it tonight. Won't distract you, will I?'

'I shan't allow you to. I get absolutely engrossed in what I'm reading.'

'Okay. But before you settle, I'd better tell you something you've evidently missed, though you'd get to it before long in Olivia's diary. She didn't have only daughters. She had one son, called Duncan, after the first MacIntyre here; they were also sure he was going to inherit the gift of an eighteenth-century ancestor, quite a famous Gaelic poet, one Duncan MacIntyre, sometimes known as Donnacha Ban nan Oran, who was out in the '45 rising and was later imprisoned for writing a poem against the proscribing of the wearing of the tartan. Because even at eight little Duncan could write quite credible verse. He died at nine. It nearly killed Olivia. It's all there in her journal. She writes so well I'm inclined to think his talent came as much from her as any long-dead MacIntyre. There's a very poignant poem in the diary that marks the turning-point in her overwhelming grief. It was sent to her from one of the clan who emigrated to America. You'll come across it. Well, I'll shut up now.'

For two hours they maintained a strict silence. Faith was grateful. She finished drawing up her plan for the next lot of typing, made notes, checked dates, looked up the New Zealand Encyclopaedia to verify political references and local developments of the day, scribbled a few paragraphs here and there as she felt inspired. Occasionally Gareth suppressed a chuckle, or sighed approvingly, she thought. That didn't disturb her at all.

She reached out for Olivia's journal, began leafing through it. She'd already read some, but had found it so fascinating she'd resolutely put it aside till she'd gone through earlier ones because Olivia's style was so good it would rob the other accounts of their impact.

She came to small Duncan's illness ... the slight cold, the sudden fear it was going to his chest, the dread of croup, the sudden certainty that it was pneumonia ... with, in those days, the knowledge that it was often fatal. The nights she and James sat up in agonised vigil, as it worked up to its crisis, the desperate attempts to bring him through. Faith knew it was absurd, when she knew how it had ended, but she found she was wanting to change destiny, to cancel yesterday, wanted fiction, not fact, wanted the crisis to reach its peak, the fever to drop, to restore that only son to his parents.

Olivia had recorded those days long afterwards and her style had changed from a vivid joy in living to a stoical endurance. She wrote with an economy of words that wrung the heart even at this distance in time. Then came the entry,

'I thought I should never write in these pages again, never know the release of words, till James's cousin in America sent this poem to me. She didn't know who had written it. It was published anonymously in a newspaper, and Cousin Marion said it had comforted her tremendously after the loss of her own little boy. She didn't know why it had, but from that day healing had set in. And so with me. I thanked my God that this unknown American woman had released her sorrow in words, expressing it so that other bereft mothers might know that somewhere, on a far continent, someone understood their anguish, and find comfort.'

So Faith read *Farewell to a Little Boy*.

'Honey, there will be a hoop
And hills to roll it down ...

(God couldn't give a little boy
    The burden of a crown).
He'll show you lots of trees to climb
    And where he keeps the swings.
(God, let him have a ball and bat
    Instead of shining wings!)
And will He let you sail a kite
    Up where the sky is clear,
Without tall buildings stooping down?
    Of course He will, my dear!
Now close your eyes ... I'll kiss them shut
    The way I always do ...
(I must ... I must not cry, dear God,
    Until he's safe with You.)'

Faith couldn't move when she'd read it. She didn't know how she could control her tears. She didn't want to attract attention.

Finally a small sob betrayed her. Gareth Morgan took one swift look, crossed to her, looked down at that copperplate hand, said, 'Oh, I'm sorry. Perhaps I shouldn't have put you on to that tonight. It's too soon after losing your father, isn't it?' He put a hand for a moment on the shining brown hair.

She swallowed, felt for her handkerchief, wiped her eyes, said, 'Not really. Dad had a good life and a reasonably long one, though I miss him so terribly. I'm always wanting to tell him something. We were such pals. I'm crying for Olivia. I've never had a child, but I've got an imagination. One feels if only one could bring the past forward into the blessings of the present day. Now, we don't have the same long vigils beside the bedside in cases of pneumonia. Anti-biotics, like mini-miracles, would have averted that crisis, the long strain on lungs and heart. Oh, the other day I was deep in these chronicles and found myself envying the folk of those days, their simple life, the unspoiled beauty of their surroundings, the virgin forests, the unpolluted seas and rivers, but there was a price paid for it.'

Gareth Morgan drew an upright chair towards the desk, said, 'You'd better read the next page or two. My mother loves it. She lost a child too, even with all modern medicine ... and, unlike Olivia, her husband didn't keep watch with her. He was down at the pub.'

Faith looked down, managed to focus.

'And now autumn is here, and the treacherous spring, and the first Christmas without little Duncan is over and gone, and today as the gulls swooped and soared above the tussocks on the cliffs, I thought kite-flying time had come again and in the glint of their wings against the sun I could imagine I saw Duncan flying his kite over the meadows of heaven. And I was able to think how lucky I am to have had all I have had, four daughters and a son. I've known anguish and travail and bitter loss, but I have also known the joy of looking upon one's son's face for the first time, seeing sturdy little limbs chasing fleecy white lambkins, have known the joy of seeing him inherit my love of poetry. These things are imperishable. For this, I give thanks.'

The grey eyes looked into the tawny-brown ones so close to hers. How would Glen have reacted to a moment like this? She knew. He would have said, impatiently, 'Oh, come. It was over and finished with at the beginning of this century.'

Then, quite unexpectedly, Gareth Morgan said, 'You know the other night when Philippa Meredith, as Tamar Pengarth, was standing at that window and said what she did, it reminded me of this. It was so crazy. I felt as if I wanted Olivia to hear her. How strange when I resent Dad's first wife so much, but for a moment I felt that Olivia and Tamar were one. Ridiculous really when it was nothing but clever acting. Oh, give the devil her due, it was *superb* acting. So she really did have a gift ... being able to portray that as she did ... a woman who never bore a child.'

Faith couldn't speak. She wanted to cry out, 'But she *did* bear a child ... me. Julian's daughter and your step-sister.'

He got to his feet, said lightly, 'Well, after all that drama, I don't reckon you can call me Mr Morgan any longer. Make it Gareth, will you?'

At that moment came a tap on the door and Aunt Chassie came in. She said, 'We wondered if you were ready for your cuppa now. The film's over. But if you want to go on we'll bring it in here on a tray.'

His voice was crisp, matter-of-fact. 'No, we'll come out for it. I've been going over some of the stuff she's roughed out. I've given it my seal of approval. How's that for patronage from a horny-handed son of the soil?'

CHAPTER FOUR

FAITH was finding great compensation in the work she was doing for the family, *her* family. They would never know, but in its finished form, it would be her dearest possession. Work was joy and even if at the end of the day she felt depleted, at least it meant she sank into deep slumber every night.

She pulled a purple sweater with a polo neck over her dark-blue jeans, came out of her room and paused as always to smile at the picture of her great-grandmother, Olivia MacIntyre. A very good photographer of the old days must have taken this, and it had been coloured with the skill of a true artist.

Hope had told her that as girls when they'd read L. M. Montgomery's *The Story Girl* they'd been enchanted with her description of her Aunt Olivia. She said, 'She was described as "just like a pansy—all velvety and purply and goldy". Mother was exactly like that. She had that strange dark gold hair, and eyes so brown they were almost purple. The only one of us to have her colouring was Prudence, Julian's mother.'

Every morning Faith saluted her forebear. She ran on down to breakfast, singing. Who could have dreamed that in just being where her forefathers had laboured, conquered the swamp and tussock, and raised a gracious dwelling amid pastoral surroundings, she would achieve such happiness? Only the bogey of her relationship to these people cast a shadow.

As she reached the bottom stair and the last line of her verse she heard it taken up again, in whistling, and looked up to see Gareth running down after her, pulling a huge heather-knit farm jersey over his head, from which the muffled tune was emerging ... 'O, who will o'er the downs so free, O who will with me ride?'

She paused, looking up, laughing. His tousled head emerged. He grinned, said, 'Good choice for an early morning song, Faith, and it's the day I hoped it might be. It's prophetic. You're not to shut yourself up in that caravan today. You're coming round the entire estate with me. The aunts are worrying lest your attention to duty upsets your health. We had a conference on it last night.'

She looked up at him saucily. 'And you've lost your fears of me since you know my affections are engaged! Thank heaven for that. We're almost like brother and sister now.'

He disregarded that, said, 'Good. I'd an idea we might have to argue you into it all through breakfast. You can tell yourself it's in the interest of the work, anyway. I feel you've gone far enough on the records, but you're not tackling it from the right angle. You're mapping out what Euphemia and Duncan saw when they breasted the hill for the first time, from their own rather bald diaries. You're seeing it with the eyes of your mind, and not in reality. You only know the views from this old homestead, you've got to be able to describe it all. You haven't as much as seen the new houses yet, or the Blowhole or the far cliffs of Goblin Head.'

She shrugged. 'But only at the end of the book will I need to describe the new, Gareth, and from what I've read of Phemy's and Duncan's tree-planting, it's not now the views they had. Hardly a skyline here but has its crest of trees. Then they would be bare hillsides. Except where the native bush clothed them. Or did the bush reach the tops?'

'That's what you've got to find out. You can only do that by seeing for yourself the bleached stumps of *totaras* and *ngaios* and *miros* and so on. Once they were black with charcoal, lying in the gullies. The first settlers had to burn off to be able to sow pasture. Sure, they planted English trees to bring autumn to an evergreen land, and to allay homesickness, but to get the true feel of other days you must know every contour of the land. Aunt Hope tells me you've admitted to being a pretty fair rider, so we'll take the car as far as the other houses. I've got Diogenes up there and you can have Troy, Rowena's mare. Megan's Atalanta's a bit dicey for a newcomer. You've got to be used to her.'

'For goodness' sake, you did go in for classical names in the stable, didn't you? They sound more like racehorses than farm horses. But why, in heaven's name, Diogenes? It suggests meditation, not speed.'

He chuckled. 'Because we lost him when he was just a foal and found him curled up in an old tub on its side. Atalanta lives up to her name with a fair turn of speed, but she stops so suddenly when she sees a succulent thistle, it's most disconcerting. We've all had a tumble from her—except Megan herself.'

'And what's your father's mount's name?' She had an insatiable thirst for information about Julian.

The answer almost made her betray herself. Gareth said, 'It's Pippa. She's gone now, died of old age quite a few years ago. By that time the girls were at boarding-school and Dad didn't bother with another. Said he'd just exercise theirs.'

Pippa had been the name the young Julian had called Philippa. She could hear her mother saying that. 'We were so happy at first. He called me Pippa. No one else has ever done that.'

Chassie opened the kitchen door, 'Time you young ones had your breakfast.'

Hope said, firmly setting down bacon-and-eggs before them, 'Now, no bedmaking, no dishes. You should be away in the pride of the morning.'

Gareth cocked an eye at her. 'You know full well, Aunt, that the pride o' the morning means a short early shower. And we don't want one. It's just your love of a nice phrase. But yes, we're going to be off as soon as we've eaten.'

It swept over Faith that his acceptance of her would have been very different had he known her true identity. She pushed that thought behind her.

As she got into the Valiant she burst out laughing. Gareth looked a question. 'You're so right about your aunts loving to use certain phrases. They throw them about all over the place and I'm terrified I get them into my notes. Honestly, when they first interviewed me ... if you could call it an interview, when it was obvious they'd made up their minds I was to come, it was hilarious. Hope actually said they knew that any morning now they could wake up in another world, and if the history wasn't compiled, they'd have a *lifetime* of regret! How I didn't guffaw into the phone, I don't know. Oh, I do love them.'

They headed towards the south boundary track, over the downland towards Waikouaiti, first taking the poplar avenue where the blue sea beyond shimmered diamond-bright between the dancing golden leaves.

Gareth looked up at them. 'I'm glad the wind's hardly more than a zephyr today. At this stage I feel like trying to hold time still. It'll take only one gale-force wind to strip the leaves now, then winter will be on us.'

Faith said, 'But winter has its own loveliness too. I'd never do for the tropics where there's so little change. I love the tracery of bare branches against winter skies, even if I shiver.'

'There speaks the blissful ignorance of one born and bred in the warmer north. The winds here, Faith, swoop up like demons from the South Pole across unsheltered leagues of the Pacific, to beat against these cliffs. See how those *ngaios* on the edge lean away, all gnarled and stunted. That's why we built Lilac Bend on the north side of Maru Hill, same as the homestead is in the lee of Bield Crags. Bield means shelter in Scotland, in Maori it's Maru. So we're snug in the houses, but as we ride round the paddocks in June, July, August, we really battle the elements, so you may change your mind.'

She laughed. 'You're wrong about being born and reared in the warmer half of the North Island. I was born in London, and when Dad wrote that book about the Shetlands, we spent an entire winter there. He set it against polar storms in an area where the shelter, if it existed at all, was mainly rocks and hills, almost treeless. And I found it bracing, exhilarating, poetic.'

'I grovel. I'm always doing it to you. You'll have to put it down to a stick-in-the-mud farmer who hasn't travelled, not understanding a cosmopolitan like Faith Charteris. Maybe I've lived too restricted an existence.'

She shook her head. 'Not really. Nobody with a library such as you have in your own room—Aunt Hope permits me to make your bed now my own passes muster —has a narrow outlook.'

He drew the car up. Perhaps to show her some features of the coastline stretching below them? But he turned to her. 'Thanks, Faith. I feel I've redeemed myself some in your eyes, after all.'

Her grey eyes searched his. 'What do you mean, Gareth? Redeemed from what? When did you blot your copybook as far as I'm concerned? Oh, surely you don't think that because you were cross about getting your car scratched I'd hold that against you?'

The tawny eyes looked frankly into hers. 'No, not that, but I had the strangest, yet strongest feeling that when I expressed myself as I did about Philippa Meredith, you disliked it intensely. It may have seemed hard to say I was glad someone was dead, especially of an actress loved by so many, but her callous treatment of Dad really ate into me. He's such a splendid person. Gran—Prudence —once told me he went through hell in the best years of his life, neither married nor free, and vowed he'd never fall for another woman, ever.

'Then he met Mother, through me, and admired and loved her. They were meant for each other. I've always regretted that they didn't meet in the spring of their lives. I'd have liked Julian Morland to be my father. The girls were too small to remember all my mother went through with my own father. You've never known anyone so abominably selfish! But I knew. I remember. I once came home unexpectedly early from school. I heard Mother crying in a way I hope I never hear another woman crying as long as I live. I stayed in the hall. She whimpered, Faith, like a hurt animal. Then the sound ceased and I heard her cry out in prayer, "Make me strong enough to bear it, God. Make me strong enough." Kids aren't great theologians, but even at that age I recognised it for something out of the ordinary. She didn't pray for deliverance from that problem, just for strength to cope.

'Years later I heard a sermon on the usually hackneyed subject of the Prodigal Son. This preacher stressed the difference between the boy who ran away and the one who came back. At first his request was, "*Give* me my portion?" On his return he asked, "*Make* me as one of our hired servants." That explained my mother to me. And she *was* given that strength. She saw my poor weak father through to the bitter end. Then, thank God, she met Julian Morland. She had some very happy years, quite unclouded. But I can only guess what it meant to her when my father's exquisitely beautiful first wife switched from films to television and she had her home invaded by her, week in, week out, year after year.' He turned his hand out in a sort of helpless gesture. The longing of a son to square accounts for a brave and loved mother.

Without thinking Faith took hold of it. 'Gareth, I think you've magnified it. Oh, I like you for it, but her happiness with your stepfather may have been so great it's ceased to matter. I think Philippa Meredith's beauty may have worried you, but a lot of that, at her age, could have been skilful make-up. That picture of your mother on your bureau shows her as no less beautiful—that tawny hair and laughing eyes. I guess her happy nature more than compensated Julian for the temperament he'd no doubt have had to deal with in Philippa's young days. Who's to know that every time he sees her on the screen he doesn't think what an escape he had, remembering the quarrels they had over her career?'

He'd never know what it cost her to say that.

He turned round more, brought his other hand to clasp her free hand, said, 'Oh, Faith, thank you for making me feel less of a heel. And for listening. I've never told anyone else, ever.'

She said slowly, 'You see, a girl as young as she was when she married wouldn't have been able to judge for herself how strong within her was this desire to act. Her real mistake was in marrying so young. She ought to have tried her wings in London first, but a strong infatuation can destroy one's judgment. It blinds us. But *true* love is, as Barrie says, an extra eye that shows us what is most worthy of regard. And Gareth, you've a chivalrous name and you live up to it in your solicitude for your mother. If you could find it in you to extend that to poor Philippa Meredith too, you mightn't see her as just someone who reached the top, but who must have carried a load of remorse all her life for the way she treated her young husband. Your own mother, at least, had the matchless satisfaction that she coped, in a very wonderful way, with a very tough situation. And she had the joy of children, which Philippa lacked.'

His grip on her hands tightened. She looked up again and had to look away swiftly, to the view beyond.

He said, 'Thanks. I believe that for the very first time I've got this tangle into the right perspective. And soon, when *The Pengarths* finishes, I'll forget it. It will be over.'

Over for him, yes, but for her, the daughter of Julian and Philippa Morland, never over. She looked back at him, ready to switch this poignant conversation back to everyday levels, but he wasn't quite ready yet.

The side of his mouth quirked up whimsically. 'I certainly read you wrong, Miss Faith Charteris. You're very different from those other empty-headed girls my dear, dilly aunts were always wishing on to me.' He looked at her consideringly for a prolonged moment, then added, 'Serves me right! I'll bet you longed to smack my face at our first meeting when I came out with that.'

She grinned. 'I did. I'd never felt so primitive before.'

'And,' he said, no laughter in his voice now, '*you* had to be spoken for!'

Faith held her breath. She was visited with a whole cavalcade of feelings, a sense of being caught up in something she must avoid, the knowledge that she mustn't involve herself too deeply, a scalding sense of regret that really alarmed her with its intensity. Wisely, she said nothing.

Their eyes met again. His were searching. He said quietly, 'I suppose that still holds good, Faith? That although you're not wearing a ring, it's near enough to an engagement?'

In a moment of painful revelation she knew why she felt like this. But it wasn't possible, any attachment between the son of her father's second wife, and the daughter of the first one he so resented.

'You suppose right, Gareth,' she said quietly.

Under his expert fingers the car sprang to life, they drove on, breasted the rise, said inane things about the view from the cliff-top, then headed for the other side of Maru Hill and dipped down to the lilac-rimmed drive of the new house.

'Not new any longer,' said Gareth. 'We've been here twelve years. The girls don't remember much before living here. There was such a gap between us because of Mother losing our little brother. There's the married couple's bungalow beyond the stables. His wife comes over to Lilac Bend every few days to air it.'

He took her through the house, built on ranch-lines, in cedarwood boards and Oamaru limestone, with wide patios and spacious rooms. Leonie must have loved this after all her insecurity. Gareth's room was just a sunroom as he lived most of his time at the homestead. She wondered if that was to give Julian and Leonie more time on their own, as much as to have a man in the house for the aunts.

They had morning tea at the married couple's house. John and Matty Bruce were delighted to see them and strolled out to the paddock with them. They already had the horses saddled. Troy was a dapple-grey. Matty said admiringly as Faith swung up, 'Exactly right for you, Faith. A purple and blue rig-out and a grey mare.'

Gareth burst out laughing. 'Women! I remember Mum persuading Dad into a car that shows country dust far more than the one he wanted, because it was the exact shade of a new suit she'd got for a wedding. As if she'd wear only that when she took the car out. But yes, it's charming, Faith. As for me, how glad I am my corduroys are brown when Diogenes is a chestnut!'

It was so long since Faith had been astride she knew she'd be stiff next day, but it was exhilarating riding along, backs to the breeze, looking northward past the mouth of the Pleasant River up to Shag Point and beyond to even catch a glimpse of the Moeraki lighthouse. Thoughts of Moeraki brought back London Airport to her, and Mark telling her where Goblin Head was situated.

They cantered over the sloping ground beneath the crags that had given it that name since pre-European times. Even as close as this it looked like a recumbent goblin. The height shut off the view of the sea. 'I'll take you round the other side of them on foot some day,' said Gareth. 'It's wide enough to ride round but forbidden because one shy or a stumble and you'd be two hundred feet into the sea. We'll skirt round and finally come to the beach near the homestead. Have you ever trotted horses in the water?'

'Only in surf. The still water of a bay should be better still.'

Here they lost all view of the dwellings. There were steers grazing, Herefords with chestnut coats and white faces, and countless Corriedale sheep with haughty faces, and snowy fleeces. This terrain suited sheep who liked to climb.

They slowed to a walk to enter a path that wound through the native bush. 'Gently does it here. Certainly we keep the lower branches lopped, but haste is foolish.' The grey dropped behind the chestnut. Faith looked about her appreciatively. 'Imagine having a whole wood to yourselves! I shall just love exploring here some day ... on my off-times.'

He turned his head, grinned. 'Don't treat me like a boss. I'm not likely to crack the whip. Come when the weather's perfect and the sun sifts through the trees and dapples this white limestone dust like a tiled floor. Ah, nearly through. Not far to the beach now.'

Scimitar Bay was curved, befitting its name, and the sand was white rather than golden. There was a trellised boat-house covered with ivy geranium still covered with pink blooms, *manuka* clustered close, gnarled *ngaios* leaned over grey rocks, garden seats under them. The ribbonwoods, those magic trees that gave an illusion of spring-in-autumn, with their frail apple-blossom-like clusters of flowers, whispered softly overhead as the horses picked their way down. Troy and Diogenes headed straight into the water, then wheeled to race along the shore, in the shallows. The sun blazed directly on them from the north, and suddenly, for the first time for months in Faith's life, the world seemed joyous and care-free. She would enjoy today, and tomorrow and all the tomorrows she could spend here where her ancestors had lived and lóved. Till she must leave, her task accomplished, her love for Puketaipo encompassed in a book called *The MacIntyres of Goblin Hill*.

They came up from the shore along the ribbonwood track, the breeze from the south stronger now, bracing and free. They dropped to a walk as they neared the house.

Gareth gave a shout. 'Oh, Gran and Granddad are here. That's their car. I rang and said they'd better get out here as soon as possible. They retired in Oamaru, because Prudence is not only part of the more recent history of Goblin Hill but she's practically a reincarnation of Olivia, her mother.' He stood up in his stirrups and hallooed.

Almost immediately there were sounds of activity, doors banging, voices calling to each other, and a figure appeared on the front verandah. Not that it stopped there. It positively hurtled down the steps and ran across the lawn to the little path through the shrubbery. By the time they had dismounted, it had nearly reached them.

Gareth was laughing. 'What did I tell you? No one in the least like a grandmamma! Robert has lived fifty years of marriage almost, in mortal fear she'll break every bone in her body. But she bears a charmed life.'

He swung down. Prudence Morland reached him, lifted her face for his kiss. How true it was ... allowing for modern dress, and a very elegant hairdo, Prudence was as like her mother's portrait as anyone could be ... a pansy, all velvety and purply and goldy. Her hair was almost white, but streaks of that strange dark burnt gold showed in the coil at the top of her head where a tortoise-shell comb caught it in place. Her eyes were so dark they had a purplish tinge, heightened by the fact she was wearing a tailored trouser suit in mauve, and her brows were beautiful, dark, even though not darkened. Her complexion was a girl's one, with a little flush high on the beautiful cheekbones.

Gareth said, 'Meet my madcap grandmother, Faith, Mrs Morland.'

Faith wanted to cry out, 'No, *my* madcap grandmother,' but that was the last thing she could do. Prudence Morland turned fully to Faith, standing with Troy's reins in her hand. The pansy-dark eyes blinked, and Prudence said, 'Goodness, child, I thought my sisters were seeing a likeness they wanted to see because your name was Faith, but they're right. You could be a Mac-Intyre.'

Faith had to take it lightly. 'Gareth's just been telling me I have the same colouring as Faith had. Likenesses are always occurring, aren't they, in the most unexpected way?'

Prudence nodded. 'And of course your own father, Stephen Charteris, had grey eyes, hadn't he? But he was a bit darker.'

To Faith's look of surprise, she added, 'Oh, yes, I've met him. Your mother too, but long before you were born. They used to visit the—someone we knew in Oamaru.' There was just that faint hint of hesitance that gave Faith the clue. Of course. Her parents had known Philippa's parents in Oamaru. They were gone long since.

Prudence took hold of Faith's hand. It trembled in hers a little. She said, 'You've given my sisters a new lease of life—we've always wanted the history of the family written, and it ought to have been done when we had the reunion for the family centenary. A hundred years from the landing at Port Chalmers, but the locusts have eaten the years. We're going to stay at Lilac Bend for a week or two because Gareth's planned a few sessions of remembering for us. We'll sort of fill out Mother's diaries for you.'

Gareth was surprised. 'You're going over there? Why? You'd be much better on the spot. There's plenty of room. You can continue the reminiscing from breakfast till supper.'

'Well, dear boy, I may be a chatterbox, but at least I know it, and also know no writer could stand it. We don't want Faith walking out on us. Can't believe our incred-ible luck to have Stephen Charteris's daughter doing it for us. Chass says she's obviously inherited her father's gift and will be famous herself some day.'

If only they knew, Faith thought, what a baseless assumption that was! Gareth said swiftly, 'Anyway, Gran, you're doing no such thing. It'd be no fun with you up there. In any case, Faith's having a complete week off from actually transcribing notes. She's just going to be absorbing!'

'Oh, are you, dear? How ideal that you should have decided on this just when we've arrived.'

Faith burst out laughing. 'Well, I hadn't. But it looks as if Gareth's decided it for me. Okay, I'm beginning to know I must just go along with this crazy family. They ought to be pushing me on to justify my wages.'

Gareth cut in. 'That's utterly illogical. It's not just a typing job. You've let out far too much about Stephen's work to get away with that. What about those weeks, even months, on some locations? In fact, Gran, that's why I've got Faith out with me this morning. I said she had to know every cranny of Goblin Head to write about it authentically.'

Prudence looked innocent. 'Oh, was that it? And here was I thinking it might have been pure pleasure for you, Gareth, not duty.' Mischief lit those dark eyes and for a moment Faith felt she'd glimpsed the child Prudence who'd been the pickle of the family.

Gareth tossed that ball back. 'You can take that matchmaking look off your face, Gran darling. Faith's spoken for. I have it on the best authority . . . from Faith herself.'

Prudence was also childlike in the way she showed her disappointment. 'Well, the girls might have told me. I've had such a happy hour dreaming you'd met your ideal girl at last. Name, disposition, interests, the lot. And I thought Julian would love a daughter-in-law called Faith. I'd talked to him so much of my adored older sister that he always hoped he'd have a little girl of that name some day. The girls didn't say you were engaged, dear.'

Before Faith could answer, Gareth did. The drawl was back in his voice. 'It's not an engagement. It's merely one of those understandings. I've no time for them. Makes for too much latitude on each side. *I'd* want to be sure of my girl.'

Prudence looked horrified. 'Gareth, you take too much on yourself. Sometimes it'd be a lot better if a girl, or a man, didn't rush into an engagement too quickly. Perhaps Faith wants to make sure before she commits herself. It's sensible.' She turned to Faith. 'My dear, you'll think us dreadful, discussing your affairs like this. I'm afraid we've given to this sort of thing. As a family we rush in with hobnailed boots where angels would fly over rather than even tiptoe.'

Faith chuckled. So did Gareth. Prudence looked relieved. Faith sobered, said, 'Well, there's so much hoo-ha goes on in all the media at present about people not being able to communicate with each other, it's a relief to find folk without inhibitions. It's another way of saying you care what happens to people. And as I've no family now I like it.'

Again the stab of longing to make herself known. *But you are my family, though you'll never know!*

Prudence beamed on her. 'From now on you're one of us. We won't have to watch what we say. It's so frustrating.'

Gareth groaned. 'It's on your own head, Faith. You don't know what you're letting yourself in for.'

Prudence turned on him. 'You're just the same. You know you are. You couldn't be more like us if you were a MacIntyre.'

'It's catching, that's all. Before I got absorbed into this family, I walked delicately, like Agag, not in hobnails, Gran, we'll ride down for the mail before we come in for lunch.'

They swung into the saddle again. Faith knew some muscle twinges as she did so and predicted more to come.

'Main thing is to keep at it now, Faith, after so long away from it. Too much sitting won't do anything for you.'

'I can see what Mrs Morland meant. This is sheer bossiness.'

'Families always boss each other round. Better than living in a lonely please-yourself vacuum.'

As they dismounted, he said, 'Well, even if I got a clip on the ear from Gran for saying so, I mean what I said about not liking understandings. I'm a yes-no person myself.'

'I can see that. But occasionally it takes time before one utters either. Common sense, like Mrs Morland said.'

'Common sense!' His tone was scornful. 'When did common sense light any candles?'

'What do you mean?'

His mouth was wry. 'You'll probably give me the slap I didn't get the other day, but here goes! You haven't got the look of a girl in love.'

He took her silence for offence. 'All right. I've gone too far. But sometimes people marry simply because they think the right one will never dawn on their horizon. They make do with a lukewarm affection.'

She looked up at him. 'I'm not offended, Gareth. I mean what I said about liking people to care enough to butt in. Only——'

'Only what?'

She shook her head as if to clear it. 'I don't know. Nothing's black and white to me any more.'

He put out his free hand and touched hers on the reins. 'Sorry. Your world turned upside down recently, didn't it? You haven't even got a brother. Take this for brotherly concern, Faith. Don't ally yourself with someone you aren't sure you love, for the sake of security. For a home to replace the one you had with your parents.'

He saw her eyes blur. He put his arm about her as he might have done to one of his kid sisters, patted her shoulder, said briskly, 'I'm probably setting up doubts where they needn't exist, clumsy oaf that I am. This Glen Tankerville—can't he rig up some excuse to visit the Town Planner in Dunedin? Or get away for a long weekend? Feel perfectly free to ask him here for a few days. He probably hates you being away down here. Look, I'll write to invite him if you like—that way he'd be sure of his welcome.'

How was she going to get out of this? Be vague, put him off? She had a flash of inspiration, remembering something that was fact, not fiction. 'That's awfully good of you, but it'd be rather a long way to come ... thirteen thousand miles. Glen's just off to London on business, taking in the States and Canada too. That's why I don't mind being away just now.'

He turned to the mailbox and left the probing. 'Two or three here for you. Do you want to read them here in the sun? Better chance of doing so here than up at Goblin Hill with four of them remembering the past, flat-stick! Ah, talk of the devil, here's a letter from your Glen.'

It was face down with the address on the back. He turned it as he handed it over, then gazed, surprised.

'Hasn't he got this address yet? It's gone to your Napier address marked "Please forward." You've been a bit lackadaisical, haven't you? It's a wonder he's not had a call put out for you.'

He took Faith's heightened colour for anger, not em-barrassment. 'Oh, aye, I'm at it again. Sorry, that's your business.' Then, irrepressibly, 'But it's what I say ... no candles! I know you've been writing pioneer history all day, but surely plenty of love-letters have been written burning the midnight oil? You ought to have let the poor beggar know where you were.'

She was stumped. She couldn't think of one reason why a near-fiancé wouldn't have her address. Talk about hon-esty being the best policy! If only she'd never been tempted into saying she was spoken for! She'd done it only to set a cheeky stranger back, but had been glad later when it had turned out he wanted no reminders of his father's first wife here, much less her daughter!

Finally she said slowly, 'Gareth, I can't explain this. It's

86

entirely between Glen and myself. Neither do I want to set you back, which would negate what I said about appreciating this family's concern for me. Would you let it go?'

She had no idea how forlorn her air or how bleak her eyes were. Gareth pushed the rest of the letters inside his shirt, pulling up his jersey.

'Right, little sister. Off you go.'

The aptness of the designation almost brought the tears again. He'd never know how nearly true it was.

CHAPTER FIVE

SHE was about to meet her grandfather! It seemed incredible that nobody knew but her. She mustn't count on him being another kindred spirit like her grandmother. He mightn't have Prudence's outgoing nature. He might be withdrawn, even shy.

He was standing in the doorway looking for them, almost a giant of a man, as tall and as broad as Gareth. He still had a touch of copper in his hair and the bluest of eyes. How strange, she thought fleetingly, that my father and myself reverted to the brown-haired, grey-eyed Duncan MacIntyre.

Gareth said. 'Well, here's Faith Charteris, Grandy, the paragon the aunts have no doubt been singing praises about ever since you arrived.'

Robert's broad face creased into a grin. 'It ought to be a compliment, but nobody likes being called a paragon, you daft lad. I'm going to call you Faith. It's a name that belongs here. Gareth, if she'd been a lazy lie-abed and had a tongue dipped in vitriol, the girls would have endowed her with all the qualities of the angels for her name alone. But they've let me read her first chapter, which was a rare cheek, I know, m'dear, so I know by that alone you're the right girl in the right place. Come away in, lass.'

He was all any girl could wish a never-met-before grandfather to be. Faith's ear detected an accent different from the Scots intonation the aunts and Prudence had retained.

She said, 'I've not delved into the origins of the name Morland yet, because I'm not up to there, but are you from the Lake District? Is it possible the name came from Westmorland? But it's your voice makes me think it.'

'Very likely. I was born in New Zealand, but my father came from Kirkby Lonsdale in Westmorland. They farmed on the banks of the Lune. I daresay I've a trace of it in my speech, for in my early days in the North Otago back country, we were an isolated family unit. Didn't go to school till high school days. We were educated at home. But it's not an easy one to pick, like Scots or Irish. How come——'

She laughed. 'I suppose Dad trained my ear. He had to have these things for the flavour of his books. He wrote one about the Lake District. We stayed for weeks at Walnut House on the slopes of Skiddaw, above Lake Bassenthwaite—Cumberland, though, not Westmorland. Do you know of it?'

The blue eyes lit up. 'Do I? Lass, this is famous! Prue will be delighted. Yes, we know Bassenthwaite, but more than that, we actually stayed at Walnut House ten years ago. We looked up relations nearby, but there were so many that rather than offend any of them by staying with others, we took rooms there. We tramped all over Skiddaw.'

Faith felt moved. If only she'd known when she stayed there that her grandparents had looked out of those windows, mounted those stairs ... she said eagerly, 'Did you notice it was built in 1716, the year after the 1715 rising? I remember feeling quite excited, thinking it would be nearly thirty years old when Prince Charlie raised his standard at Glenfinnan.'

Her grandfather took it up. 'And you wondered if he passed that way, to or from Carlisle? So did we!' He took her by the arm, marched her into the dining-room. 'Prue, Prue, guess what? She stayed at Walnut House in Cumberland. And she knows Kirkby Lonsdale and banks of the Lune. After dinner she and I'll sit down and have a grand old yarn.'

Gareth, on their heels, guffawed. 'Aunts ... you're

stonkered! Grandy's got you beaten. We're off the Mac-Intyres and on to the Morlands. Faith, you'll never get away from Goblin Hill. Make up your mind you're here for a long time.'

Robert said, 'Oh, she's got to be here when Julian and Leonie get home. They'll love talking over the Lake District with her. Our son was always so enamoured of the Lake Poets, Faith—Wordsworth, Coleridge, Southey. So they spent a long time there and stayed at Walnut House too. I'll give you the letters to read. Anyway, you'll be able to stay for ages, won't you? I mean you can do the final typing down here, can't you? You don't want to rush back to Napier, do you?'

Before she could answer, Gareth did. 'Well, that depends upon how long she can stay away from her beloved. She's all but engaged to a town planner. But rest easy now, Grandy, he's safely in London at the moment.'

Oddly, for that loquacious household, a silence fell upon them. Faith was aware her perceptions were heightened, that these dear encounters with her own kin had added some quality to life not known before. Because she sensed that a shadow had fallen on them. They would like her to stay. And but for Gareth, she would.

Then Hope said flatly, 'I keep forgetting that, Gareth. But I do wish you'd stop reminding us of it all the time. Let's just live in the present. I've got the strangest feeling —as if Faith has always been here.'

'That's because of her name,' said Gareth. Was his tone a little harsh? Strange, if so, because he was so gentle, even if teasing at times, with the aunts. Then he added, 'I'm starving, I don't know about you, Faith. Let's wash and get at it!'

The Morlands stayed on at the homestead. Faith felt the happiness of each succeeding day assuaged the sense of loss that had swept over her when first Lucy, then Stephen, had left her alone in the world. She was no longer alone. Even just the knowledge that she belonged to this family coloured every day.

They'd already said she must come back often, even when she was married, for holidays, and bring her husband. Well, there wouldn't be a husband, certainly not Glen! He'd be a danger, he knew who she was, and he had no finer feelings. Besides, he was right out of her life now. That was all washed up.

Hope and Chass, Robert and Prudence knew not only the estate history but the district history too, because even Robert, from the time he was nineteen, had worked here. They made it come alive for Faith. She'd known the history of Otago only in the way she'd known other distant provinces in her schooldays. The Hawkes Bay history she'd grown up with, and had researched it later, for Stephen.

But these dear people had learned their local history by word of mouth from the first MacIntyre of Goblin Hill. They even sketched in pre-MacIntyre history, taking her out to the south headland where Waikouaiti lay spread below, and drew that colourful past so skilfully for her that Faith could almost see the whales surfacing and spouting and gambolling in the unsullied water of the Pacific ... the whale-boats putting out, the incredible bravery of those who hunted down these glorious creatures in their frail-looking boats; could see the trypots on the shore, the amazing network of the organisation needed to take these products to the markets of the world in the days before that world shrank.

Then the colonisation of New Zealand, and Johnny Jones, to become a legend in his own time, seeing the opportunity and extending what became almost his own kingdom. There was his wise decision as whaling declined, to bring men and families to this far-flung shore, to set them up in farmsteadings of their own, giving each man sixty acres when he'd worked there two years to prove himself.

He became a sort of feudal baron, a man of vision,

quick temper, equally quick to admit his fault, a hard bargainer, but one who despised the chance to make money out of scarcity and resisted the temptation to raise prices to make a fortune for himself.

Then came the time when Euphemia and Duncan travelled up from Dunedin, negotiated for their own land, faced incredible odds in clearing the richly forested downs and headland for grazing, not wanting to follow in Johnny Jones's footsteps, but longing to create a smaller estate where generation after generation of MacIntyres might follow.

Though Duncan had been dust in that little kirkyard on the hill beyond the railway line for more than half a century, the reverses he had suffered and surmounted tore at Faith. These were her people and their pain was her pain. How poignant for Euphemia to bear all those sons and finally, at the turn of the century, to have only one left, James. It smote Faith with anguish. One son lost his life trying to rescue the crew of a fishing-smack wrecked off Goblin Head; one died in infancy; two didn't come back from the Boer War.

James had known his son would be the sole MacIntyre of his generation, and even that, when small Duncan had died, had come to naught. How glad he must have been when Prudence married one of the estate men and they had produced Julian.

Now Julian's stepson would inherit and he would call his son Duncan MacIntyre Morgan. At the thought Faith had to clamp down on her wistfulness. God grant he did have a son, even if no MacIntyre blood would run in his veins.

Robert made every landmark clear to Faith with incidents connected with it, and the diaries underlined every one for her. Even those early days that concerned the district rather than the family were dear to her. Looking down from here she could see in her mind's eye the port of Waikouaiti booming as the gold-rush hit Central Otago and men from other gold-rushes, in California and Australia, flocked here in their thousands, landing here to head into the almost trackless wastes inland, via Palmerston and the Shag Valley, right to the Dunstan.

As the gold fortunes fluctuated, other industries arose ... coalmines at Shag Point, a rabbit cannery at Dunback, dairies, bakeries, cordial factories. Grain had to be ground, horses had to be shoed, blacksmiths' shops sprang up everywhere, waggons had to be serviced, accommodattion houses provided.

Into the port came the colonial-built shallow-draught wooden schooners and cutters, then steamers. Paddle-steamers made their way from Dunedin and back, for the seaways were still the best means of travel. All the time the MacIntyres devoted their lives to the land, not swayed by excitement or the chance of making money quickly on the lawless goldfields, but sowed and reaped, threshed their oats to feed animals, sold their mutton to the gold-hungry men on their way. Not all of it was profit. Duncan and Euphemia never saw a man go off ill-equipped to face the hazards of a barren wilderness, of snow and tempest, or the rapacity of the traders who followed them to make riches out of dire need.

Horses were bred, some sold to miners and, later, to the waggoners who, as the country became more settled, were the lifeline between the Hawkesbury and Dunedin. Rivers were bridged, cuttings made; the railway forged south from Christchurch but was long delayed because of the ruggedness of the country from here south. Faith felt she shared the thrill of the settlers when the first train from Christchurch to Dunedin ran through on September the sixth, 1878. What a day of rejoicing ... another barrier to the comparative isolation was ended. But now ships called less frequently.

The MacIntyre land was cut by the railway. They received compensation but suffered much inconvenience till, in later years, the viaduct lessened the tedious work of moving stock through railway gates.

There was little cash to spare. They lived off the land and sometimes didn't see the colour of money for months on end. In between times clothes were cut down, turned and turned again. Sheets that wore thin were turned sides to middles, the children's underwear was made out of flour-bags, with the names bleached out of them, sometimes their shirts too. Handkerchiefs were contrived from salt-bags, beautifully hemmed. Their jerseys and socks were from the bits of fleece caught on the barbed-wire fences, spun, carded, dyed and knitted by Phemy herself.

Then came comparative prosperity. The homesteads held more parties. Families intermingled in marriage. Euphemia rejoiced when James married Olivia and found in her the daughter she had longed for, and when Faith was born to them, the old house rejoiced indeed.

The twins added to the joy, and when small Duncan was born, Euphemia and Duncan knew the glad hope that the name would, after all, carry on. In any case, then, they had two other sons who would marry, have families, not knowing that they would die with the horses that had been foaled and bred at Goblin Hill, on the lonely veldt. Prudence had been born on Euphemia's seventieth birthday. Before she was a year old and while little Duncan was a sturdy-limbed little farm lad, the pioneer couple were gone.

Despite the tears Hope, Chass, and Prudence often wiped away, through it all emerged a pattern of philosophy, of courage, laughter, and a strong faith.

Chass said, her blue eyes wide with remembrance, 'Then war broke out in 1914—the Great War. Oh, the scenes of fervid patriotism, Faith, even in this small community. By the time World War Two came, people knew war for the horror it really is, though they still responded to the call when Britain's back was to the wall. But World War One was a fever in the blood.

'The whole land was affected. From the most remote parts offers of money and horses poured in to the Government. In the Capital a great assembly of Members of Parliament, Cabinet Minsters, the Prime Minister and the Governor-General looked out from the Parliamentary steps upon a moving mass of twelve thousand citizens, singing and cheering. When the announcement of war was read out they broke into the National Anthem, followed by *Rule, Britannia.* That fervour reached here too.

'My mother sent me, one day, with a message to my father. I found him in the stables. He didn't hear me coming. He was stroking the muzzles of his favourite horses and saying, "I'm loth to send you, my bonnies. The men know what they're doing and have decided to make the sacrifice, but you don't. You were born and bred to peaceful pastures and the freedom of the paddocks, but now you've got to face the heaving of the sea, and rigid training and—and shellfire. But I'm too old to go myself, and my only son is dead. But—forgive me, my bonnies."

'I didn't make any more noise going than I had coming, and I sped back to the house and flung myself on my mother and howled my head off. And when she'd comforted me, she gave me a piece of bread-and-jam and sent me off to find Faith and Hope and went herself to the stables.'

Grand forebears she had, thought Faith proudly. 'And then,' she prompted. 'When it was all over, what then?'

They hesitated. Then Prudence said, 'That's enough of yesterday's sorrows. Chass has filled the flasks. We're going down to the shore to remember other, happier days when we had the big family picnics, the bigger community ones, the races run on the shore when the tide was out, the lolly-scrambles in the turf above it. When we went hunting crabs and rock-oysters and swam in sun-warmed pools all day. Because there was a larger sum of happiness than ever the sum of sadness amounted to ... but we're inclined to recall the tragedies because they're the stuff of which drama is made.'

Gareth joined them for the picnic, smelling of sheep and hay, and very glad to relax. He and Faith climbed the Tower Steps. Every feature had a story. This one had dozens, mostly imaginative, because it was here Olivia had brought her daughters, to act out the tales of derring-do they were so addicted to. They had been steps to German castles on the Rhine, ladders to the stepless doorways of Border keeps, the girls gazing out like imprisoned maidens incarcerated for loyalty to the men they loved, rather than marry the suitor of their father's choosing.

Here Prudence had been the Maid of Neidpath, chanting from Walter Scott's poem, 'Though now she sits on Neidpath's tower to watch her love's returning.'

Here Rapunzel had let down her golden hair ... twine teased into a long plait, and a neighbour's son, trying to climb up it to Chassie, had first nearly pulled her over because it had been firmly attached to her belt, then had slipped himself and broken a wrist. Despite that he'd had the courage to marry her fifteen years later ...

'But our worst escapade,' said Prudence, 'was when we got too realistic about Scott's lovely Rosabelle. Chass and I stood on the steps chanting,

"Moor, moor the barge, ye gallant crew!
    And, gentle lady, deign to stay!
Rest thee in Castle Ravenscleugh,
    Nor tempt the stormy firth today."

'And Hope, down below, got all carried away and pushed the dinghy into the water, meaning to go out only a few feet, leap into the shallows and drag the boat ashore. Dad never left oars in, to stop us doing such things, and she got carried into that little eddy over there and sucked out between the rocks and swirled out of the bay.'

Chass said, 'I'll never forget it. We had the sense to know one must keep the boat in sight, so Prue took off to get Father. I reckon he broke the four-minute mile to the shore. He got the other boat out and had just rounded the point when he met a fishing-boat coming in, with the dinghy in tow and Hope on board, very cock-a-hoop. She'd recovered from her fright and was immensely enjoying being made a great fuss of by everyone.

'Father never said a word to any of us till they all reached the bay and were ashore. Then he spanked the three of us well and truly. We were humiliated. But worst of all, we were halfway through *Rob Roy* and he didn't let us read anything of Scott's for a whole month!'

The Tower Rock was a natural formation with an aperture in it like an arrow-slit, through which the luckless maidens gazed out to sea, hoping for a sight of sail to signal rescue was at hand.

Gareth chuckled, 'When those three start telling their stories, they don't know when to stop. Thought I'd never get you up here. My sisters have heard those tales over and over, but they're quite insatiable. The way they identify with the old days, you'd think they were MacIntyres too. I think Gran and the aunts often forget they're not.'

Faith pushed back her chair to cool her brow. 'You identify too, with the MacIntyres, don't you, Gareth?'

Their eyes met. He frowned, then his lips tightened. 'I can't for the life of me think why, but you sounded almost as if you didn't like that. I might tell you, Faith, it's not for the money. It may look that way, but it's because it means everything to Gran and Grandy to know that Goblin Hill won't have to be sold to complete strangers when Dad passes on. It shouldn't be for years yet, please God, he's only forty-eight. Mother's a bit older. So we're pals as well as stepfather and son. He was only thirty-three when I came here to work. We're probably closer than some fathers are to their real sons.'

She looked bewildered. 'Gareth, it sounds as if someone has twitted you with gaining a legacy not yours automatically by descent. So perhaps you're touchy on it. But I couldn't think of anyone I'd rather it went to, in the fulness of time.'

He stared. 'What an odd thing to say!'

She crimsoned, knew panic. She'd given away her interest in the property. She managed a small laugh. 'Yes, wasn't it? As if it's mine to bestow. Maybe I'm identifying with the MacIntyres too. I just mean that if the first Duncan could have seen into the future, he'd have been very happy, I'm sure, that someone like you, loving every inch, carried it on.'

There was a strange look in the brown eyes under the heavy tawny brows. He didn't say anything, just kept looking. She knew an almost overwhelming desire to hold out her hands to him. How odd it was, to be matching look for look here on the cliff-top looking north over an infinity of blue sea. It made her nervous. She must break this pregnant silence.

She said lightly, 'So you must marry someone who'll love it as you do, Gareth. Don't ever marry anyone who'd want to sell and move nearer town. Oh, dear, what a nerve! I'm as bad as those old-time fathers who chose their daughters' husbands! But it would be wonderful for your step-grands and Julian and your mother if you brought them someone with a feeling for antiquity.'

His well-cut mouth hardly moved. 'Yes, wouldn't it?' he said.

She thought it was more than time they went back to the others. Safety in numbers. She had to pass him on this narrow rock path that was hardly more than a groove on the top. 'Come on, Gareth, I'm sure they're calling us.'

'You don't think anything of the sort. It's subterfuge. Didn't they tell you the story of the Rhine sailor who rowed the maidens out to join their lovers, but exacted his own toll first? Like this?'

He caught and held her as she went to pass him. His fingers were like steel about her upper arms. She caught her lower lip between her teeth in a rueful, childish way. He grinned, quite unrepentantly, 'Loosen up, Faith, I can't kiss you like that. Stop biting your lip.' She'd never seen those brown eyes so dancing, so devil-may-care.

She said quickly, doing so, 'But—but I said I was spoken for.'

'I know. I also told you what I think about these some-time-never understandings. You seem to be havering. I thought this might help you to a decision ... now!' He bent his head and the brightness of sun and sea was blotted out as his lips came down on hers.

He must have known she was shaking when he finished. He held her as she swayed. She kept her lashes down. She dared not look up at him, she'd have given too much away.

He said, 'Did they tell you the story of the maiden who never rejoined her lover? She fell in love with the sailor.'

She said, 'If you're not careful I'll ask them if that's true.'

He chuckled. 'You won't, you know. You wouldn't dare.'

Neither of them had seen the redoubtable Prudence reach the top of the steps. Her head had appeared above the ledge they led to. She'd blinked as she saw those two figures in close embrace. She shook her head a little to make quite sure she wasn't imagining it, then smiled to herself, and began to retreat, carefully feeling for the second step down with her foot. Thank goodness the others couldn't quite see her from down below! She felt for another and another, clinging to the rock sides of this chimney-like formation. She reached the bend, managed to turn round, then called up, 'Are you there, Gareth? We're going back to the house now. Chass has just remembered Kathy's going to ring at four-thirty. Will Faith come back with us, or will you bring her back on Diogenes?'

Gareth let go of Faith, peered over, said, 'I've promised to show her Warriors' Leap. I'll bring her back.'

He burst out laughing at the outraged look on Faith's face. 'Well, if you'd asked me I'd have promised.'

'I've seen it—from the other side, with the girls. Where

the invading Maoris came in from the sea, in mist. And the gallant defenders here took them as they scaled the cliffs and plunged into the sea with them to keep the women and children in the fortifications safe. They know I've seen it.'

'Well, I didn't want to go home yet. Thought we could have continued this pleasant dalliance.'

'Dalliance! It was hardly that. Really, Gareth ... if anyone heard you!'

'Well, Glen's thirteen thousand miles away, so he can't challenge me to a duel, and if it wasn't dalliance it was certainly pleasant. For crying out loud, hark at me ... you've got me talking in the parlance of the Middle Ages!'

'*I* have? It's not me. *I'm* only sunk in pioneer days. It's *you*! You've got carried away by languishing maidens and rescuing knights and cheeky sailors. All right ... show me Warriors' Leap in case you think the girls didn't do it justice, then we're going back. I might get Prudence to tell me beyond World War One while others get the dinner.'

He stopped in his stride towards the Leap. 'No, not tonight, Faith. Not with everyone there. Gran wants to tell you the rest on her own. Recent history's a little too painful. She's afraid she might break down. She asked me to tell you.'

'She must indeed think of you as her own when she'll tell you that. Some women her age would hesitate before confessing that to our generation.'

'Perhaps, but then she knows I love her dearly.' He grinned. 'I believe I'm forgiven for my cheeky behaviour just now. I thought I'd really blotted my copybook.'

'Oh, are you apologising for it, then? If so, I accept. And I'll forget it.'

'Could you?'

She was too enraged to answer.

The smile was still in his voice. 'Anyway, I wasn't

apologising. You can only apologise for something you're sorry for. And by heaven, girl, I'm not sorry.'

'You'll be jolly lucky if I'm even speaking to you by the time we get home,' said Faith crossly.

It had no effect on him. 'You *do* think of it as home, don't you?'

Dangerous ground. 'Well, it's where I live at the moment. But home is really where the heart is.'

'In that case, yours ought to be in England, where Glen Tankerville is. With the Town Planner. But I could swear it's not.'

Anger warmed her cheeks. 'Gareth! You go too far. How dare you belittle anything as important and artistic as Town Planning? Country people can be snooty. So many folk just have to live in cities. Some long for beautiful surroundings and can only achieve it if people like Glen can create it for them. When you talk like that you're not only getting at him, but also at designers. Someone may have written: "I think that I shall never see a poem as lovely as a tree", and I love trees passionately, but imagine London without St Paul's! Perhaps a man can create as much loveliness out of stone and mortar as out of sapling and seed!'

'Whew! I feel as if my eyebrows have been absolutely scorched off! I'd hate to be up against you in a debate. You think of such things! You do remind me of Gran. She turns us inside out too at times.' He said persuasively, 'Come on, Faith, do forgive a horny-handed son of the soil his arrogance, his clumsiness. Starve the lizards, you've got me grovelling again! I shall finish up a worm. If I have to go to a psychiatrist to have my inferiority complex sorted out, it will be your fault. I'm not as bigoted as I sound. There are three things that stir me greatly, Faith ... a slender sapling staked against the gales, that will become an enormous beech a hundred years from now, the sight of Knox Church spire against a blue Dunedin sky, and a printed page with a poem on it. A poem *can* be as lovely as a tree.'

She liked him for that. Oh, *how* she liked him. Liked *and* loved him. That should have added up to the ideal, but couldn't, because twenty-six years ago, her mother had put a career before her husband.

She managed to grin at him. 'All right ... you've erased the blot, you dolt. Remind me to show you a poem in one of Dad's scrapbooks some day. It's dedicated to an architect. Now, let's go. I'll walk back. I love ambling up that track.'

'Oh, no, you don't. They didn't call me Gareth for nothing. It's up with the lady across my saddle-bow and off. You'll find it quite comfortable.'

She did more than that ... she found it disturbing, fitted against him, his chest warm again her back, his knees tucked in at the back of hers. He held the reins with one hand, let Diogenes pick his way, holding her with the other. She wondered if it was necessary ... but it would be nice to remember afterwards.

When they gained the comparative level of the plateau-like paddocks he said to her, 'Can you remember that poem? You've got a great memory for poetry. I'd like to hear it now.'

Why not? She began:

'God spoke to one in cultivated fields,
  Rich pastures seamed with green and gold of gorse,
Grain heavy in the ear, a sweep of plain
  Threaded by some green-willowed watercourse.
Sleek cattle winding home, the laden boughs
  Where apples ripen, and the upturned sod
Where ploughed fields lie; all these to him, it seemed,
  Revealed the beauty and the voice of God.

'God spoke to *you* in crowded city ways,
  In cloistered arch, tall dome, and slender spire,
In gracious symmetry of wood and stone,
  Till in your heart there rose a deep desire

To build with beauty in the city's heart,
  Where weary feet for countless years have trod,
And in the joy of lasting craftsmanship
  You find the beauty and the voice of God.'

Her voice died down the stillness of the fields about them. She knew his silence for appreciation. Then he said, '*You* wrote that, didn't you, Faith? That's why your father kept it?'

'Yes, I wrote it.'

'It was published?'

'Yes, in an English magazine.'

He said, as one stating a fact and not asking, so she didn't correct the wrongful assumption, 'And you wrote it because some awkward chap—like me—was a bit scathing over Glen's work. If he feels like this about architecture, then perhaps from his designs we'll get more of the old style buildings, not these wretched blocks of flats that square our skylines and cut little children off from all contact with the good earth. I take back what I've said about Glen. If he could inspire a poem like that from you, with your love of sea and sky and trees, then I needn't fear he's not the chap for you.'

Just as well for him to think that. It had been written to a friend of Stephen's. He had taken them round the Backs at Cambridge one blue-and-gold-and-rose day in June. He had talked of his ambition to so design modern churches and colleges so their lines wouldn't date, but would stand the test of time as these had; and would never be despised by future generations as the products of a grotesque age.

CHAPTER SIX

PRUDENCE suggested the little summerhouse for their next session. 'Gareth said he'd told you why I'd rather be alone. The epidemic of 1918 must be mentioned in this record, but I don't think Julian's disastrous first marriage need be. Gareth has told you of that, he said.'

Faith's eyes were a little bleak. Those years of her father's life were to be skimmed over, as if they had never been. Perhaps there'd be a brief mention of his course at Lincoln College, then his marriage to Leonie and a reference to the fact that in time his stepson would carry on at Goblin Hill. What a pity to end a magnificent family history on such a note!

The summerhouse was on a rise above the garden, reached by rock steps, and looked north over Scimitar Bay. It had been erected for Euphemia when she had been away in Dunedin once, as a surprise for her.

'It marked the first extravagance Duncan felt justified in making,' said Prudence. 'The honeysuckle and the cottage roses may not be the very same ones she planted, but they are cuttings from the same stock, renewed generation after generation. I find that comforting. Life is like that, too.'

They sat up at the small octagonal table that matched the structure. Faith's ballpoint moved so swiftly it was not distracting. She needed just an outline and would fill it in later. Her methods made for a full flow of narrative.

'You said the epidemic must be mentioned ... when the world was swept with influenza.'

'Yes. It seems so incredible to remember now. Antibiotics were unknown. It was a real state of emergency. I'll never forget the empty desks in our school classes when it was over. Doctors were rocking on their feet, so were undertakers. Faith had married at nineteen, in 1913, before the shadow of war fell on the world. She and Harold were so happy. He left here on the outbreak of war and survived the hell of Gallipoli, but was wounded and sent home. Faith nursed him back to almost perfect health. He helped Dad on the farm—there was no other labour to be had. It restored him.

'People went down so quickly. When parents succumbed neighbours had to take the children. Our house was full of youngsters, and Mother was wonderful with them. Faith and Harold did fantastic service nursing the parents, going from house to house all round the district. They seemed to bear charmed lives. Then I caught it. Mother said Faith and Harold virtually pulled me back from the gates of death. But they were so tired. When they went down with it, nothing could save them. They died on the same day. I owed my thirteen-year-old life to Faith and Harold.

'My little boy Julian said some day he'd have a little girl and call her Faith for the aunt he never knew. I'd laugh and say his wife might want to call her baby by her own favourite name and that it was a girl's due when she'd gone through childbirth for the first time. But he always used to assert that the girl he would marry would like that story too. That it would come to pass. Aye di me, there's a lot of water gone under the bridge since then, and he never had a daughter, much less the chance of calling her Faith.'

Faith wanted to cry out: 'But he did, he did, and however badly his wife treated him, at least she called his daughter by the name he wanted.'

Prudence said, 'He was such a dear little boy. Oh, that sounds just like any fond mother, but he was so confiding, so engaging. But sometimes I wonder if I should have brought him up in a tougher way, more able to discriminate, perhaps. He was so idealistic ... too much so for his own good ... very like our Faith in looks and nature. But it didn't bring her the sadness it brought our Julian. We were sorry he was an only, but he had all the boys on the farm to play with, sons of the estate workers, and ever so many girl cousins, so he grew up able to share. Then he went away to Lincoln ...' Prudence stopped.

Faith said gently, 'Dear, Gareth has told me the story of those years, as you know. Don't harrow yourself with it now. You said it's not necessary to the story, not fair to Julian and Leonie. I know this book is just being privately printed for distribution among friends and relatives, but those years are better skipped, for their sakes.'

Then Prudence said a surprising thing. 'Not just for their sakes, Faith, for the sake of Philippa's memory too.'

Faith made a little sound of surprise. Prudence said, her smile widening the sweet contours of her mouth, 'Faith, Gareth has this thing about Philippa because of his mother. He resents her with every inch of his being. Perhaps when this series is ended and he knows she'll never appear in another, he'll get over it, but I can't feel that same personal animosity towards her, even though my son suffered so much through her. Till Leonie came to Goblin Hill, bringing us all great joy. But when you think of the thousands, millions even, who see her on television and thrill to her acting, it makes one wonder if she should have been judged by ordinary standards. So it wouldn't be right to smear her image. Besides——' she was still smiling a little.

'Besides what?'

Prudence turned her hands out in a sort of mystified gesture. 'Faith, I could never quite hate her. You see, I couldn't help liking Philippa. So did Rob. That, in a way, hurt us most. We just loved her. Rob fair doted on her to start with, felt she was the daughter we'd never had. He went all quiet on it, wouldn't talk about it, for once, and I couldn't somehow reach him. He couldn't quite believe she'd gone for good. But it would never have worked.

'They were just impulsive young things and very much in love. I don't think Julian ever recognised the burning urge, the compulsive need in Philippa to act. He took it for granted she'd come back to the farm with him, settle down. She didn't realise, in turn, how rooted Julian was in the soil. She saw no reason why they couldn't go off to England for a few years for her to try her wings. If Julian had been anything but a farmer, it could have worked—say a teacher, or a clerk or something. We were still in our prime and not likely to retire for years.

'I've often wondered if we should have sent Julian after her, and if they'd had a family might it have been different. She just might have wanted a more stable sort of existence for her children than the background of the theatre and returned here. But I doubt it, because all that latent talent was there and she knew it. It was oil and water. Yet that first year in Christchurch when they were both studying, they were so happy it lifted the heart to see them. Perhaps it was only a gossamer happiness, not likely to last, but at least my boy had that.

'I went up there once and saw them, in the spring-time, wandering along the river-bank, hand-in-hand. The sun was shining through the blossom on a cherry-tree, all radiant and transparent. They didn't see me, and I didn't interrupt. It was too idyllic. It reminded me of a poem in my old booklet of New Zealand verse. It was by Alma Chamberlain and she'd called it *Youth*.

"Tread gently, for the cherries are in blossom,
   Like gossamer, a-quiver in the sun,
So frail they seem that careless winds would crush
    them,
   Tread gently, little one.

Tread gently, as you wander up Life's highway,
   In radiant Youth, enraptured and aglow,

So fine a thing, a careless step would spoil it,
Tread gently, lest it go."

'I think they found the next year more difficult. Neither would give way. So Philippa took ship for England. Julian had to carry on alone. He was still just a lad in years, but not in experience. It was like a miracle when Gareth came to work for us and we invited his mother and sisters up for the school holidays. She'd suffered too, in fact even more than my lad. She took his broken life and welded it together again. He just worships her. It was wonderful to see that idealistic look back in his eyes. She's never once let him down.

'Even when Philippa went into TV work and appeared so constantly on our screen, only Gareth resented it. Oh, Leonie must have had her moments, but she didn't show them and I think she conquered them because she felt so secure in Julian's love. I feel she named her son well. Gareth has a strong sense of chivalry in him. His mother was breadwinner for so long. She took on a fulltime job so she could put him through university. She knew she'd never have the money to put him on a farm of his own, but if he'd gone to Lincoln or Massey, he might have become a lecturer in such things. He'd begun to work here in his school holidays. But nothing his mother could say or do moved him from his resolution to leave school and come here permanently as soon as he was fifteen. He said it was time he took over the responsibility of the family, that she could now take a part-time job and stop driving herself to death.

'Then that miracle I spoke of happened. She and Julian fell in love—a lasting love. We built them the ranch-house because I feel all couples must be on their own, and there was the family to consider too. But the girls and Gareth already loved Julian and there were fewer corners to be rubbed off than there might have been. He's found all he ever dreamed of in Leonie. They're pals as well as lovers. Their interests are identical and they each appreciate the other the more because of past disillusionments.

'And recently, when I knew Leonie had taken Julian down to see Philippa, I thought it was wonderful. Leonie wrote us in detail about it. Said Philippa had been very perceptive—she hadn't dressed up for it, and was in baggy old gardening slacks and flat-heeled shoes when they arrived. They thought Mark Denby was the kindest person and ideal for Philippa. She said in her letter, "Well, Mother, I thought it tidied things up nicely when Julian said to them, 'I'm glad my wife had the courage to do this. We were two foolish youngsters, Philippa, not at all suited, and the ensuing years have straightened things out very nicely for us both.'"'

'The only regret Leonie knows is that she never gave Julian a child of his own. A complication after the birth of her younger daughter had ruled that out. But I told her we weren't fretting, that who was to know if Julian's son, had he had one, would have wanted to farm? I don't believe in trying to live our lives over again in our children and grandchildren. And I believe that some day a small Duncan MacIntyre Morgan will farm these acres. I feel it in my bones.'

Faith gathered her papers together, stood up. She went to Prudence's side, said, putting an arm about her shoulders, 'I don't wonder Julian didn't stay bitter, with a mother like you, Mrs Morland. The bit I like best is that you didn't harbour hate against the woman who turned your son's life upside down.'

Prudence put a hand up and patted the one that lay on her shoulder. 'Thank you, my dear. I'm not an angel, though. I tried to hate her and couldn't. And, Faith, you uttered no word of blame either. Nice to find a young girl so understanding. Mind if I say something personal? In a way it's why I told you so much. Looking back on that marriage it's easy to see why it couldn't last. So, in your own life, do remember it's so fatally easy to make a mistake. Make quite sure that the life this Glen Tankerville leads is the one that will satisfy you. If you truly love him it won't matter, even if it may never be easy. But ... search your heart. You might find more kindred interests elsewhere.'

That was as far as she could go. She must leave it there. Faith stood quite still. The inference was plain. Not only the twins were matchmakers. Prudence had seen her son's life torn by marrying someone who did not love the land. They had talked this over. They saw in this girl who bore their loved sister's name an ideal wife for Gareth. One who loved the rolling pastures and the old homestead and its treasures, who had a feeling for the past, and was bringing the family saga within the pages of a lasting record. If only they knew! Because although Gareth was attracted to her, he was looking forward to the day when constant reminders of Philippa Meredith no longer intruded in his mother's and stepfather's lives. And if he knew who she was he would send her away before her father returned.

She felt as if Gareth just bided his time. There was no follow-up from that challenging embrace on the cliff-top when he seemed to be demanding that she should contrast her feelings within his arms, with her attachment to Glen.

She'd been surprised to see that first letter from Glen. He had said he'd like to see her on his return from Europe and would contact her then. Meanwhile he'd look forward to her answer. She'd let him wait, then wrote saying he didn't seem to understand she didn't want to pick up the threads of her association with him again, ever. That she had visited her forebears' estate, found they wanted someone to write the family history for them, so was here compiling it. However, she'd felt that it could be disturbing to them to mention who she was, and this brief contact had satisfied something in her, but she would be moving on when this was finished and hadn't even decided whether she'd stay in New

Zealand or go to live with Mark Denby in England—he was, after all, her stepfather. And she would wish him well in his career.

All sorts of tantalising possibilities came to her mind. She even toyed with the idea of telling Gareth she'd decided not to marry Glen Tankerville and then, if he *did* ask her to marry him, keeping her own counsel about her identity. But each time her common sense rejected that. If he found out, ever, he'd accuse her of gross deception, lose faith in her. It *could* come out ... Glen and his mother knew, for instance. His mother might, some day, succumb to the temptation to tell some gossipy friend this intriguing item about a world-famous actress. No, Faith, don't play round with any idea you could get away with it. Finish your job and depart.

The jottings were finished. It wouldn't have the ending she would have liked, but that was impossible. She had the expertise, gained from her work with Stephen Charteris to know where, under these circumstances, it should end. Better for those who would read it to have it ending with Julian, Euphemia and Duncan's great-grandson, still farming Goblin Hill.

Now she had the material collated she knew it was too good to be just issued in a private printing for local distribution. Unknown to the family she got in touch with a Wellington publisher she knew very well. He was most enthusiastic on the telephone. 'I've got to be in Oamaru and Dunedin on business in a week or two, Faith, I'll drive in to visit you. They need not know it's about this book till I've had a look at it. I think even the name Faith Charteris on the jacket would be a selling point.'

Faith knew the happiness of being able to do something for her dear family all unknown to them.

There came the night when the phone rang in the lounge. Gareth said, rising to push the mute button in on the television set, 'Answer that, Faith, would you?'

The operator's voice, seeking to confirm the number, said, 'This is an international call, from Canada, and a person-to-person one. Mr Julian Morland is calling Mrs Robert Morland. Is she there, please?'

Faith felt her heart jolt against her side. Oh, if only it hadn't been a personal call! If only she could have heard her father's voice asking for his mother. It would have been so sweet. But she said, 'Yes, Mrs Morland is right here, I'll call her.'

She turned, her eyes sparkling because of the treat her grandmother would get, said, 'It's for you, dear. Your son is calling you from Canada.'

The pansy-brown eyes looked as radiant as the eyes of a young girl. She stood up, her knitting tumbling, said swiftly, 'Rob, go to the other phone so we can share it.'

He crossed the room with the speed of a young man. They all held their peace so there'd be no distraction. They looked extremely interested too, trying to glean from Prudence's answers what it was about. She was good, repeating leading phrases, so they could get the gist of it. Faith saw them relax as they found out he was evidently just phoning for the sheer joy of hearing their voices. Nothing was wrong.

In turn each was called to the phone, the twins sharing their listening as Prudence and Robert had done. Julian and Leonie were evidently snatching the phone from each other. When they spoke to Gareth, Faith knew an almost overwhelming temptation to rush to the extension.

Gareth was sweet with them both, said, 'Yes, I can imagine that by now you're both longing to be home, but don't yield to impulse yet, dearly as we'd love to have you. Make the most of every moment. Don't come back wishing you'd seen more.' Then, surprisingly, he spoke her name. 'Faith?... yes, she's here. I'm sure she'd love to speak with you.' He turned. 'Gran and the aunts have sung your praises so much, Faith, they want to thank you for all you're doing.'

She felt her heart just racing. Her ears drummed, then she managed to steady down. Leonie said, 'Oh, Faith, we couldn't leave you out, dear, so greetings from the land of the maples. I wonder if, in your travels with your author father, you've seen Canada?'

Faith told her she knew it from two visits paid from England—yes, it was truly beautiful. They exchanged delighted comments on mutual places both loved, then Leonie said, 'There's something I must ask you. Please, please don't on any account leave Goblin Hill before we get back?'

Faith caught her breath. 'Why?' Leonie answered. 'Because Julian is sure nothing his aunts or his parents will tell you will reveal how much they themselves did for the estate and family. They exalt the ancestors and play down themselves, so he wants to make sure justice is done. Do promise you'll stay? Doesn't matter what it costs. Besides which, you seem to have brought a fresh lease of life to them all. We've never had such happy letters.'

Faith knew gladness flowering within her. How wonderful to be asked to promise such a thing. To be here when her father returned! She promised. Leonie said, 'Here's Julian now.'

Faith was glad she had her back to the room because her eyes were misty. A man of direct speech, evidently ... he wasted no time on preliminaries, said, 'Hullo, Faith ... how truly wonderful to be able to speak that name to someone at Goblin Hill. Makes me put your coming there down to Providence. I feel as if for my mother, today has rolled up like a screen and given her happy yesterdays. I endorse all my wife has said. You've no pressing need to go before we get back, have you? Oh, good.

'It almost unsettled us knowing that at last the family history is to be put in a permanent form. There are certainly things to go in that the others would hold back out of sheer modesty. Gareth's letters have been a joy to read. You seem to have the same flair for unorthodox adventure my darling dilly mother has. You must have made some impression when Gareth could speak of you so glowingly after you'd dented his brand-new car! Yes, he told me of that inauspicious start ... every little detail.'

(No, Father dear, he won't have told you one detail. He wouldn't have said he'd thought I was a man because my first name is Meredith.)

She managed a laugh. 'They're all undeservedly complimentary because they somehow imagined writers were feckless creatures sitting head-in-clouds all day, chewing a pen, and having no conscience towards dishes and meals. They've made me very much at home. I must go, Mr Morland, this must be costing you the earth ... anything else you want to say to the others?... oh, just good-night to them all. Yes, I'll see you when you return, goodbye.'

She spun round from the phone and had no idea that her eyes were so starry they all wondered. 'What dear, crazy, extravagant people,' she said. Gareth suddenly got to his feet and strode out. Faith looked after him and frowned. 'What's wrong?'

Prudence said, 'Let him be. I expect hearing his mother's voice was a bit much for him. Men don't like to show their feelings.'

Faith said, 'No, most men don't, but Gareth isn't one for hiding his, I've found.'

Prudence looked at her and burst out laughing, but all their questioning wouldn't make her say why. Wild horses wouldn't have dragged from Prudence Morland what she'd seen on the Tower Steps the other day.

Faith knew a deep contentment. The situation mightn't be perfect, but as least Julian and Leonie wanted her to be here when they came home, so she'd have that to remember, weeks spent in company with her very own father, writing the history of his—their—family.

Days were full. Faith spent hours in the dormer room they used as an attic. It was full of old photographs, bric-à-brac, letters that revealed endless incidents else forgotten, stiff taffeta frocks, splitting in their folds, yellowed lace collars and cuffs, mittens, feather boas, dance programmes, fans, things that had added elegance to a raw, new world. Gareth used to laugh to find her there, her brow dusty from the hands that swept the shining brown hair away from it, eyes full of dreams as she unearthed the past.

He discovered she'd been well trained in the art of the camera too. She set up many a hitherto despised relic to photograph it for an illustration. She said now, looking up at him despairingly, 'I've got so much material it's sheer agony deciding what must be discarded. I ought to stay away from this dormer. I no sooner decide my jottings are all complete when I think of some treasure up here that ought to have a mention, and even what I've already got typed is the approximate size of Gibbon's *Decline and Fall*!'

He considered that, dropping down to the floor beside her. She was sitting cross-legged, a pad on her knees. Chaff fell out on to the page. She looked up, laughed, said, putting up a hand to his thick tawny hair and brushing it, 'You look as if you've had your head in the chaff-box with the horses.'

He grinned. 'Troy turned round and blew at me just as she took her head out of it. Thought I'd got it all out. Regular hayseed, aren't I?'

She laughed. 'Only externally.'

He took her up on that. 'What do you mean?'

She looked away. 'Oh, hayseed conjures up someone bucolic. With not much more in mind than threshing oats or hoeing turnips. And——'

He prompted her, 'And——?'

She shrugged. 'Just that you're so learned. There's hardly a subject crops up but you seem to have some knowledge of it.'

115

He grimaced. 'Purely from reading. No one in a world of books needs to limit his mind, even if he did have to leave school at fifteen.'

'Correction, Gareth. Even if he left school at fifteen. You didn't have to. You chose to, and in so doing, gave your mother the best life could have offered her.'

She saw the colour creep up under the tanned skin, but knew from the look in the brown eyes that he was pleased. He said, 'Oh, I don't look for any bouquets for doing that, Faith. In doing that I gave myself the life I wanted.'

'But you'd have liked Lincoln first, wouldn't you?'

'Yes. But except that I'm conscious at times of gaps in my knowledge, there were great compensations.'

'I'm sure there were. I've not noticed any gaps that matter. Your reading capacity alone might be something any university student might envy. You were free to choose what you wanted to read. There are some things in varsity life many students would rather be without. But I'm glad you didn't go through life with a chip on your shoulder because you missed out on that. It's something one has to guard against. It's so easy to feel self-pity, not only for the things one gave up of one's own freewill, but the things that cruel circumstance denied one.'

He looked at her curiously. 'Do I detect a note of longing in that? What circumstance are you wistful about, Faith?'

She didn't answer. He said impatiently, 'Oh, Faith, come on! You know all the MacIntyre and Morgan secrets. Do you always have to withhold something from us? Is it because you were an only child, born to your parents late in life, and didn't even go away from home to work? So you can't seem to confide in your contemporaries. I believe you'd rather talk to Gran than with me, about your own life.'

She said slowly, 'I—I believe I *would* find it easier.'

He pushed the pad off her knees, stood up, pulled her

to her feet, held her wrists. The brows were down, the eyes keen under them. 'There are times when you make me very angry, Faith. Not angry *with* you, but angry *for* you. There's something wrong and I'd like to know what it is, only you don't trust me. It gets me. You're fighting something. You seem so much alone, so forlorn, despite Glen Tankerville. Come on, grant me the privilege of—of a friend. Tell me.'

She looked down, bit her lip. It was true. And she would give anything to tell him—but he was the one person who couldn't help her. She mustn't be tempted.

He said, 'It's hard to understand such reticence when right from the word go I turned myself inside out to you.'

'What do you mean?'

'When I told you how I felt about Philippa Meredith, remember? When I said how glad I'd be when that series ends and my mother won't have to live in her shadow any longer. I quite surprised myself—it's not the sort of thing one reveals to someone newly met. But I did, mainly because I didn't want you using your first name. And that was in the first half-hour of our meeting. You'd think by now you'd feel you could tell me what's bothering you, what chip might have settled on *your* shoulder. But you only accept confidences, never give them.'

A bleakness swept over Faith and was apparent. He looked at her, hopefully. In a moment of utter loneliness and honesty she just might give utterance to whatever was eating into her.

He saw her visibly take hold of her slipping discipline. She looked at him frankly, though. 'Yes, something does get at me at times, Gareth. Can't you imagine why I don't let myself go? Because it's something that isn't *my* secret alone. It concerns someone else, and if I gave it words, I'd hurt the person I love most in the world.'

Oh, why had she said that? Meaning she'd hurt Gareth Morgan, and his mother through him?

His lips compressed, lines grooved themselves in his

tanned cheeks. 'Then that leaves me with nothing to say, Faith, if it concerns Glen. They told me to tell you lunch was almost ready. But if ever you do feel the need to put it into words I hope you'll look on me as the one to come to.' He paused and added rather flatly, 'As a brother, I mean.'

As Faith went downstairs with him shoulder to shoulder, she knew an anguish. Not for herself alone, but because she knew he too was experiencing this oneness of spirit, recognised something in her that she recognised in him. But she was the one who knew it wouldn't, couldn't work.

Before they entered the room Gareth said, 'Just as well the girls arrive for the holidays tomorrow. They're such a madcap pair that complexes and guilt and inhibitions simply melt like ice in sun.'

She wondered why he'd used the word guilt. Because that was exactly what she felt. She ought not to be here, Philippa's daughter!

It was true about the girls. They filled every moment to the brim, leaving no lonely hours for doubts. It seemed to Faith as if it marked time for them, as if this was a loving interlude, full of fun. The aunts insisted that Faith took a break.

Faith said, 'I bid fair to be spoiled. Most typists work as long as I do. It's hardly slave labour.'

Hope said shrewdly, 'But most typists just copy. You're doing creative work, which is much more exhausting. It must drain you of vitality. Weaving facts into a readable book must be a colossal task. You're overdoing.'

'I endorse that,' said Gareth. 'Besides which, if she takes time off to be with the girls, it'll leave me free of responsibility for them. But mind, Faith, no making up time at night. Every time you go out on Troy for an hour you disappear at night and make it up. A guilt complex.'

Faith pulled a face. 'I am being paid for this.'

Chassie said, 'Ah, bah! It's not a big wage, yet at times

you work like a demon possessed. Now, you've got to imagine you're just a friend we've asked here for a holiday.'

Faith grinned back, 'Right, I'll be a guest, but they don't draw wages. I'll concur if you don't pay me for a fortnight.'

Finally they agreed, thankful to have her relax.

Prudence said, 'You do need it, Faith. You have a great look of strain at times.' Prudence thought she knew why. This girl was fighting to maintain an old loyalty—not easy, that, and it was obvious she was drawn to Gareth, yet was all but engaged to this wretched Glen. Prudence hoped Faith was just biding her time till he got back to New Zealand. Would the girl then fly up to Hawkes Bay and examine her feelings, face to face with him? Life wasn't easy for anyone, least of all for the young. Even if it wasn't as definite as an engagement, if Faith thought a break would hurt this Glen too much, she was the sort to see it through.

One felt so helpless. Prudence was honest enough with herself to realise she wasn't exactly neutral. Gareth was as dear to her as a grandson of her own would have been, so if he married a girl called Faith, and one of this calibre, it would seem like fate. Robert was so set on the idea. Every night when they went to bed he referred to it. 'She's not engaged to this chap up north,' he would point out. 'It'd be a different matter if she was wearing his ring. I just wish he'd meet someone in England. This girl is so right for our Gareth.' Prudence still kept her own counsel about that embrace she'd witnessed. Robert wouldn't be able to contain himself if he knew that.

Megan, Gareth's sister, said now, 'Faith, it's so funny, you're even beginning to talk like us now.'

'What do you mean? I——'

'Perhaps you didn't notice it, but just now you said, "I bid fair to be spoiled." That's a phrase in use at Goblin Hill. I didn't notice how many expressions we'd picked up from here till we went to boarding-school and the other girls noticed it. The MacIntyres of Goblin Hill have a lingo of their own, almost. I did a project for school on a fourth generation homestead and mentioned this. It was practically a self-contained unit for so long, the life-style remained in a fairly set pattern.'

Faith sparkled. 'Go on, Megan. Good heavens, girl, if you notice things like this, you ought to have written the family history, not me. I've remarked on this in the book. I've said that you turn a page back into yesterday when you live at Goblin Head. That in many ways it's pure Walter Scott. I've quoted some examples, but you can probably add to them. Aunt Hope saying Bluey must have hurt his foot because he was fair hirpling along; Chassie not saying she was thirsty but parched; and both of them saying of their father when they'd got up to some terrible prank, "he was neither to haud nor to bind". What other things have you noticed?'

Megan said, 'When they say of Gareth that he doesn't often get his birse up but when he does he does it properly.'

Gareth was indignant. 'You might find another instance, you brat! That makes me sound a bad-tempered devil.'

Rowena said, 'But it's so true, dear brother. You've probably never seen yourself with those eyebrows of yours down and a fierce scowl on your face. I go for cover myself then. Faith, you may not have experienced him in an adrenalin mood, but when you do, beware!'

Faith and Gareth caught each other's eyes and burst out laughing. Gareth said, 'Wrong, Rowena. The first time she ever saw me was like that.'

The girls pounced. 'But why?'

'Because I'd expected the aunts' amanuensis to be a man. I was peeved.'

Faith said hurriedly, 'It was really because I'd been looking after Benjie, and when he fell in a bog, we left our buckets of fruit in the drive and he scratched his new Valiant on one. That'd make any man mad.' She wanted no reference to her first name. The girls might refer to it when their parents came home.

But something had distracted them. Megan said shrewdly, 'But you soon stopped being peeved, didn't you, dear brother?'

Gareth looked at his sisters levelly. 'You'd better squash any hopes you have in that direction, girls. Faith isn't—quite—engaged, but she's attached. To someone in Hawkes Bay.' He turned to Faith. 'Sorry about this, Faith, but better to choke my sisters off before they get really stuck in.'

Rowena scowled. 'What foul luck! We thought it was foreordained, a match made in heaven. She likes all the things we do, she's a prime favourite with the twins and Gran and Grandy think the sun shines out of her, and ...'

Their brother looked at them shrewdly. 'And you two thought it would make a fine end to the family history to bring in a girl called Faith who even has the same colouring as the Faith who died in the epidemic?'

Megan retorted, 'Well, what's wrong with happy endings?'

'Nothing, you nit. I'm all in favour of them. Of Mum's happy ending for instance. But for the love of Pete, don't try to manipulate any strings here, girls. You seem to forget that an ending like that wouldn't be a happy one for Glen Tankerville ... to lose a girl like Faith. You should just see the fat letters he writes her!'

Very neatly turned. It had the ring of finality about it. Faith had an idea the girls knew there was real rue behind Gareth's tone. Perhaps it was a good thing Glen had been so persistent. He'd completely disregarded her answer to his first one, putting an end to their relationship. It was most infuriating, but the tone of all his subsequent letters carried the inference that this was just a little tiff, and they'd carry on where they'd left off, when he returned.

His letters were full of self-importance, of how impressed everyone over there was with his innovations and ideas; he'd enclosed newspaper cuttings that mentioned him, and stressed the fact that he'd met so many V.I.P.s. The last one had even hinted he might stay in Britain. That he knew she loved Britain, that it was her second home as so many years of her life had been spent there with Lucy and Stephen and her real mother.

What did it add up to? That now he knew her birth was impeccable, he once more considered her fit to carry on the Tankerville line? Every time Faith thought that she clenched her fists in fury. But she thought ignoring his letters was the best thing to do. He'd give up eventually. But at least those letters had served to bolster up her pretence.

Gareth said now, 'Well, I must get back to my fence-tightening. You can bring me a cuppa at three, girls.'

Faith said, 'I'll get into old riding things. Let's take the horses down to the shore.'

As she went out of the room she heard Megan say in a low voice, 'An attachment. Mightn't mean a thing. There's many a slip . . .'

Faith decided to ignore it. What a fortnight followed! They filled every moment to the brim, riding, tramping, helping Gareth draft sheep, feeding out, cleaning out the stables, the fowl-houses, trucking sheep to the saleyards, getting Robert to take them fishing, staying over at the ranch-house to stock up the deep-freeze with cookies against their parents' return.

They were thrilled when Faith's publisher friend came to lunch and dinner. They felt none of their class-mates would have met a real live publisher in the flesh before. He was delighted with this remark and said he felt like a tiger at the zoo. They took it for granted he was negotiating with Faith for something of her father's. He and Faith shut themselves in the study for the afternoon and at dinner he made an announcement to the whole family.

'*The MacIntyres of Goblin Hill* is far too good for just

a private printing. The politics and changing conditions of the hundred and twenty-odd years are so skilfully woven into the quite delightful family background, so it's going to join the ranks of our books that deal with great pioneer families. I've suggested very little in the way of change. Faith worked with her father for so long it's more expert than most manuscripts of its kind. There's no doubt that she inherited his gift.'

Faith looked swiftly down. That couldn't be true, of course.

Then she looked up, her eyes sought Gareth's first, then her grandmother's, her grandfather's, her great-aunts' ... the gladness and pride she saw in all was reward enough.

Griff Meldon said, 'Charteris on the cover will be a good selling point, of course, and it's a happy coincidence that she too is Faith. A nice touch. The only thing I'm not sure of, though, is the last chapter. It's a little bit of an anticlimax. Of course she's only got it roughed out so far. But something may occur to me. I know it's not a work of fiction, to be rounded off, but I feel it needs something.'

Prudence said a strange thing then. 'I don't think that need be decided yet. Time has a way of writing our endings for us.'

Nevertheless, the problem of that ending gave Faith a white night. She tossed and turned. She thought of Stephen and how once when he'd been interviewed, he'd said that when he began a book he knew two things ... the beginning and the end. It was the chapters in between that worried him! But this book, written by the hand of experience through four generations, couldn't have an imaginary end. It had to be for real.

No one knew that the true ending could never be revealed. Because she loved Gareth too dearly to bring him any anguish.

CHAPTER SEVEN

Only in her frequent letters to Mark Denby did Faith feel really natural and sincere. She held very little back from him—in fact, only her own feelings towards Gareth. She told him that Gareth's complex about Philippa prevented her from revealing who she was, that she felt she was best to go away from here as she had come, someone who took on a job and finished it. But that she was very happy to have seen Goblin Hill, to have heard the tales of her forebears and that at least she would know her father for a few weeks. She asked Mark never to put his name and address on the backs of his letters. Those letters to her were warm, heartening. She was lucky to have such a stepfather.

Winter set in early once the girls had gone back to school. Robert expressed satisfaction. 'I like my seasons early, all of them. If we get a mild late winter, with few frosts and little rain till well on, I always feel we'll have a bad July and August, and it often carries on into September when we lamb.'

Faith said she'd never enjoyed severe weather more . . . she spent long hours in the study and saw the pile of typescript growing. It would all have to be done again, but by then the task would be less formidable because it would be so condensed. Gareth drove her to Dunedin one day to take a pile of ancient photographs to an expert to be reproduced. They visited the Early Settlers Museum together, to check on references to early implements and household items that hadn't been preserved at Goblin Hill.

They called at the school and were allowed to take the girls out to dinner and to a theatre, then, on a clear, frosty night, with stars like silver sequins in a blue velvet sky, with a full moon lighting up the whole nightscape, they drove home together, mainly in companionable silence.

The small stretch of motorway curved over the lower slopes of Mount Cargill, dipped into forested areas of pine and larch that looked purely Canadian, came out to the wide expanse of moon-shimmered lagoon at Blueskin Bay, but instead of climbing the Kilmog, Gareth turned off on the coast road past Warrington.

The moon was soon completely free of a tantalising cloud that had been trailing it and the twin curves of open sea and lagoon at Karitane that made this coastline so enchanting, showed a frill of foam against the sable shadows of the shore.

Faith caught in her breath as they crested the rise above and the full beauty of it burst upon her. She said, 'Oh, Gareth, did you ever see such beauty before? It's so lovely it almost hurts. Because we can't hold time still, and a night like this may never come our way again. Could we watch for a little while?'

His voice was suddenly harsh, surprising her. 'No, Faith, not tonight. Content yourself with this one glimpse,' and his foot went down on the accelerator.

Faith swallowed with disappointment, then said hastily, 'That was stupid of me at this time of night. It's far too late.'

He said quietly, 'That's not the reason. It's late enough, but if I'd wanted to get home I wouldn't have taken this coast road with its dips and twists. It was foolish of me. I wanted to show you this by moonlight, but now we're here, I dare not stop driving. Get me?'

She said, rather faintly, 'Yes, I'm sorry, Gareth.'

He said, 'I know you are. But I'll get over it. We met too late, that's all.'

Faith was glad when they reached home. She didn't know how to handle this. She hadn't the courage to put her fate to the test by telling him who she was. Because other people were affected. If she told him who she was and he told her to go before his mother came home, she'd never see her father, and the job would be left unfinished, the one thing she could do for her family.

Hopefully, Prudence had left out a thermos jug of coffee for them. She'd put sandwiches under a napkin, on a low table. In a tiny vase she had arranged three winter roses, perfect in their waxen purity. The fire had been banked so that it glowed red to its heart. The standard lamp had been turned on, the others switched off. They halted, gazed. Neither of them dared face the intimacy of that. Faith knew Gareth's reason. He didn't know she felt the same.

He switched the centre light on, strode to the table, took a couple of sandwiches off the plate, laid them down, handed the rest to her, and the jug, and said, 'Take these up to have in your room, Faith. I'll make myself a cup of coffee down here.'

'Thank you, Gareth,' she said, and left him.

Again the storms beat up from the South Pole, howled across the headland, but they were snug in the old house behind Bield Crags. The giant trees that had thrived so well here they almost caught up in size to their much older Northern Hemisphere counterparts broke the force of the gales and saved the garden from destruction.

For a week they were house-bound except for the men riding round the property or working in the blacksmith's shop or the sheds. The aunts begged Prudence and Robert to stay on. 'When the house is full it's like the old days, and it's so easy for Faith to refer to you for confirmation of things we've forgotten.' Faith was glad to be free of the temptation to be outside with Gareth.

On the worst day of all, Gareth spent most of his time in the homestead. Faith had called out for Prudence to help her unravel some anecdotes and they struck a problem with time sequence. Prudence finally called Gareth in. This had to be correct as it concerned the Hawkesbury district rather than the estate. Finally Prudence left them to get on with it.

Faith thought she'd never known Gareth so quiet, so strained, so economic of words. Yet they managed to concentrate on the matter in hand and finally emerged at dinner-time with the satisfaction of knowing it would be plain sailing now.

The others seemed aware of his edginess too, because they indulged in small talk, in short bursts. Till now conversation round this old table had gone deeply because they had been thrust into the intimacies of a hundred and score years of family life and had found such kindred topics, the talk had never languished.

When they finished washing-up and came back to the fire, Gareth said, 'There's hardly a thing worth looking at on the box tonight. Pity, winter programmes are usually the best.'

Faith yawned and stretched her arms above her head. 'I do hope it's fine tomorrow. I'm stiff for want of exercise. Perhaps I should go and slide down the banisters for an hour or two!'

Gareth got up abruptly. 'Right. That settles it. I feel the same—as restless as a caged tiger. Let's put on the sou-westers and the oil-slickers and defy the elements! I can't stay inside another moment.'

Faith expected the older ones to dissuade them. It seemed sheer lunacy, but she longed to be out in the fresh air, but all Chassie said was, 'There's just one thing, Gareth, don't take her to Scimitar Bay. Take her to the south side.'

Faith was surprised. 'Chassie, isn't that the more sheltered? The south faces the Antarctic!'

Robert said, 'It's the only sensible thing to do, lassie. It's always been recognized here that it's safer to face the storm on a cliff-top. The other way you could get bowled over, but mind, Gareth, watch her. She's considerably lighter than you and doesn't know this terrain as well. Keep away from the edge. The tussock will be slippery with water.'

'I'll go nowhere near the cliff-top. We'll face the storm for sure, but from the far side of Bield Crags.'

Gareth made her put Megan's hobnailed boots on. 'It's true that it'll be as slippery as hell tonight.'

Faith grinned. 'Somehow I never think of hell as icy!'

He grinned back. 'Put them on and don't be so saucy.'

They seemed to be back on the old friendly footing. He knelt to fasten them for her, looked up. 'Bit of a come-down, isn't it ... after seeing that programme last night on the Elizabethan courtiers? The days of chivalry. Sir Walter laying his cloak in the mud for his Sovereign. And I'm taking you out in the teeth of a howling southerly in hobnails!'

'Nevertheless, Gareth, I still think they named you well. Don't you think anyone who knew you left school at fifteen so your mother wouldn't be the sole bread-winner might sometimes fancy they heard the clink of armour ... not hobnails?'

He finished his task and stood up. 'And,' she added, 'I hear it still, in the way you want to protect her from any-thing that might hurt her. From the pain of remember-ing her husband was once married to one of the most beautiful women in the world.'

His brown eyes were serious and they searched the grey ones beneath them. 'Thanks, Faith. I've always had the feeling you thought I carried that too far, that it was an obsession. And you disapproved. But now I think you understand it.'

She nodded. 'I do. I know you're always happy when that programme is over.'

'Yes, I admit that. But I don't feel it nearly as intensely as once. Not now I know she's gone and there'll be an end to it. I believe it will run out about Christmastime.'

Faith felt impelled to try to find out something. 'Gareth, could you never think of it as over and done with? Why does it remain a live issue with you?

Prudence opened up a bit to me, and she just loves your mother. It seems to me Julian and Leonie have a wonderful marriage and your mother ought to feel most secure in your stepfather's love. Why do you feel as you do?'

He considered it. 'It used to worry me to see Philippa so glamorous, so exquisitely gowned. I thought it might give Mother an inferiority complex. That she might worry lest Dad, looking at the screen version of his first love, might get unsettled.'

'Yes, I can see that. You'd known your mother's unhappy years, but now Philippa is gone, will it always worry you when some film of hers returns?'

'I can't help hoping we get none on television. If they're on in town theatres we don't have to see them. The girls will want to see every one, of course. But when they aren't home, we can switch off. I'm looking forward to next year, Faith, I feel the New Year will usher in a new era for my mother, free of reminders of her predecessor.'

As they went out into the storm, Faith thought not only the elements seemed bleak. Her future did, too. A future without Gareth.

Nevertheless, the tussle with the gale did them both good. The trees were bent away from the south, the clouds went scudding across the sky away from it. They themselves bent over, but towards it as they struggled up the cart-track to Bield Crags.

Gareth said, 'Did the girls ever take you to Clach Dhion?'

She had to yell against the screaming of the wind. 'No, what does that mean?'

'The Shelter Stone. It was so like one on the mountain farm the first MacIntyre came from. Although it faces south, it gives shelter because it's carved out by aeons of weather like a half-canoe, standing up, and there's a sort of parapet, partly natural, partly built up with rocks and mortar, so you can stand behind it and rest your arms on it and look way down to Otago Peninsula at Dunedin. Not that it will be visible tonight. But it's spectacular to stand there on a night like this, listening to the waves dashing against the cliffs, and feel safe.'

She had to cling to him as they edged round, then they were in the hollow of the rock, only their faces exposed to the lash of the wind.

'Isn't there supposed to be a stillness at the heart of the storm, Faith? I'm always reminded of that when I'm here.'

They remained silent a long time, just looking out over the streaming landscape. Suddenly Gareth put his arm round her shoulders, but didn't draw her to him. He spoke into her ear.

'Faith, there's something I'd like to know. Maybe I've no right to ask it, but I feel impelled to. Suppose you had come here before you—before you formed this attachment with Glen, might things have been different? I mean, of course, between you and me?'

She knew she mustn't admit it. This wasn't the time for her usual yes–no response. She tried to speak lightly. 'Oh, Gareth, what a question! The point is, I did meet Glen first. I've known him a long time. You've known from the start we were almost engaged. I've a feeling you oughtn't to have brought this up.'

He said quietly, 'I wouldn't have, but for one thing. I've chewed it over for a week trying to fathom it. I've had my doubts about the depth of your feeling for him for some time. And I thought it very strange he didn't have your address for that first letter. But when you quoted me that poem you said you wrote him, I thought I'd been wrong. I thought you'd never have written that to him unless he was a kindred spirit and the sort of man a girl like you ought to marry. So I accepted the fact I'd fallen for another chap's girl and there was no future in it for me.

'You said, when I was disparaging about those soulless blocks of concrete some modern architects design, that he loved the old styles. But the other week I had to wait in Oamaru for the car and filled in time at the library. I was looking through some North Island newspapers, for an article on fertilisers and in the *Hawkes Bay Herald Tribune* I saw a photo of Glen, complete with a drawing of a block of flats he'd designed for an Auckland firm. They were hideous. What does it mean, Faith?'

Nothing that could excuse it came to her mind.

He waited.

Then he turned her round to him, said, 'Faith, *did* you write that poem to Tankerville?'

She knew a deep shame. 'No, Gareth, I didn't. I wrote it to a very wonderful friend of my father's.'

'Then why did you pretend Glen was that sort of architect? I'd like a completely truthful answer. Was it because I hurt you being disparaging about someone you loved? Or was it in defence?'

'Defence against what?'

'I think you know, Faith. Defence against your own feelings. Your feelings for me.'

Again she didn't answer. Then she said, with a hint of desperation in her tone, 'Gareth, please! I don't like all this analysing.'

'You mean you're afraid of it? Good!'

She said, with a ring of truth, 'Gareth, it's not as simple as that. I don't want to explain. I told you once my reticence concerned someone else, someone I couldn't let down. I have to go away from here when the job is finished, Gareth. Don't ask me to stay. Or to explain.'

He stood there, trying to take it. Then he said, 'All right, Faith. Look, just don't move for a few moments. Let me hold you, just like this. Just stay still. I won't kiss you—that'd be too much for me. Just let me hold you.' He put his rain-wet cheek against hers, then he said softly, 'I don't pretend to understand, but I ask one thing: If ever the situation changes, you mustn't be too proud to come to me. And Faith, it's this air of guilt you sometimes wear that bothers me. Look, I know you've lived a very different life from mine and spent months at a time in some of the most sophisticated cities of the world even if you are a country girl at heart. If—if ever you played the fool a bit, did things that worried your conscience later, don't think I'd hold it against you. Or if, because of—well, some unguarded moment—you feel bound to this Glen, yet know your feelings have changed, just admit it. I'd try to understand it. So never let anything like that hold you back.'

She was moved deeply. S e stirred a little in his hold. She didn't look up. She said, 'That's pretty big. It's nothing like that, but I'll always remember you said it. It's just a force of circumstances, something I can't change. Something that means I can't stay. But—thank you for saying what you did, it's about the biggest thing a man can say to a girl, that. We'll go back now. Don't let the others know anything like this has been talked about, will you? And, Gareth, while I'm here, just let's be pals. I think we're both mature enough to achieve that.'

'We are,' he said, 'and I'll trust you, if ever the situation alters, to come to me.'

She said bleakly, 'It's nothing that *can* change, but——'

He said, 'Faith, that's too final a statement. A situation might not change, but people can change. Now, don't sorrow over this. I've had my say. You know how I feel. Let's leave it at that.'

Perhaps she ought to be glad he thought it had to do with Glen.

She was also glad she was alone in the house when Mark Denby rang her from Los Angeles. He had had to visit Hollywood on business. If anyone else had answered, and he'd given his name, they might have linked him with Philippa, as her husband and producer.

It was so marvellous to hear his voice, such a relief to be completely natural with someone. He said he was ringing because he couldn't resist it, when the Pacific Ocean he could see from his hotel window actually lapped the shores of Goblin Head. Had he had time he'd have flown over to see her, but he had commitments in London in ten days' time. 'But I'll hope to some day, darling. But perhaps you'll come over to me before then.'

He was concerned for her. He'd sensed the longing between the lines of her letters, to be known as well as loved by this family of hers. He thought that when Julian and Leonie came home, she ought to tell them, to at least give them the chance to accept this. 'If you'd met Leonie as I did, you'd know she was big enough to take it. She had no jealousy whatever of Philippa, nor had any need to know it. If ever there's a perfectly matched couple, it's those two, Julian and Leonie.'

Faith said into the phone, 'But I told you about Gareth's complex—his gladness that by next year his mother will have nothing to remind her. I couldn't do this to him, Mark. I'd always feel the cuckoo-in-the-nest.'

Mark accepted that. Then he went on, 'But my real reason for calling you is to put you on your guard against Glen Tankerville. I thought I could say this better than write it. When you told me, after Philippa died, that you'd broken it off and why, I hoped you wouldn't make it up again. He didn't show up in a good light over that. But now it seems he wants to try his luck again. It seems he's writing to you. I thought he was over-confident about you and your feelings.'

'Oh, Mark, you needn't worry. He's been most persistent with letters. I haven't answered any after the first, which just tidied things up. There's no chance of my ever taking up with him again. I know what you mean, though. He's even hinted he might stay over there, that I love England, and what about joining him? I can't think what's come over him—to be quite candid, he was never as ardent as this!'

Mark's voice was grim. '*I* know what's come over him! I've an idea this doesn't happen in New Zealand, but you've probably noticed during your sojourns in Britain that it's often revealed how much a deceased person's estate is worth. Philippa's was large, of course. You and I know how it was left. Glen didn't. Oh, he talked a lot of insincere twaddle—said it ought to be revealed that you were Philippa's daughter, that it would remove any cloud from you. I told him that seeing he and his mother were the only ones who knew, and everyone else thought you were Stephen's and Lucy's daughter, it wasn't an issue.

'I gave him no hint that Philippa had said that if you wanted to make it public any time, you could. That it wouldn't hurt her image now, and that she'd be proud for the world to know you for her daughter, if ever it was necessary and if it would give Julian pleasure. But if you decided against it for any reason, either, it would be all right. I'm glad you dumped him before you knew all this. He's not the man for you, my love.'

'I know, and not to worry, Mark darling, he'll make no headway with me. I'll probably never see him again. He'll give up soon. Now tell me, how are you, and how are things going? I think I will come for a visit, a prolonged one, when I've got this job over. It's a thrill, Mark, it's being published in New Zealand. I've always been thrilled about sharing Dad's work, but this is something I've produced almost on my own—with a lot of help from my grandparents and great-aunts, and—and my father's stepson.' She wasn't to know how her voice had softened on that last phrase. It conveyed a lot to Mark.

They talked on. She knew the cost wouldn't worry Mark.

Finally she said, 'Well, we'll leave it at that, my dear. I'll see this book through. I'll have to be here for a bit after Julian and Leonie get home, they've some material they want included that they feel only they can do justice to. But it won't be too long before I see you. It will be so wonderful to see you again. Don't work too hard ... though I guess loneliness would be eased by being busy. What did you say? Oh, how truly thrilling! Scotland in autumn would be out of this world. And how about the Lake District first? Then the Trossachs and the Highlands. Sounds idyllic. And listen, darling, always remember in your loneliest moments how dear you are to me.'

It was at that moment she realised she was no longer alone. She knew a singing in her ears. Had she—in the last few minutes—mentioned Philippa? Had she said Julian ... or 'my father'? Oh, dear God, no! Please? Mark said, 'Bless you, Faith. Philippa and I were so terrified that when you knew the truth you might have turned from her ... from both of us. We were afraid it might destroy what had been a lovely relationship between the three of us. And you've always been so sweet with me. I always looked on you as a loved stepdaughter, even though you never knew, and we saw you only when the Charterises brought you to England. Goodbye, love, and God bless.'

Faith turned round to face whoever it was had come into the room. She knew her eyes were full of tears.

Her eyes met Gareth's. He was very white. And he was angry too. Had she given it away?

He said, 'An overseas call?'

She nodded. Later she was glad she'd not said, 'Yes, from Los Angeles.'

He said stiffly, 'Well, what I heard really convinced me there's no hope for me. I'd thought something else was holding you back. I honestly thought what you felt for Glen Tankerville wasn't enough for marriage, for a lifetime. I think you ought to have made it quite plain to me the other night, up on the Crags, that you loved him ... like that! Nothing could be more convincing than what I overheard just now ... a honeymoon in the Lake District and Scotland ... in the northern autumn? Well, that's it, then.' He turned on his heel and went out.

Faith stood, one hand on the telephone table, as if carved in stone. She'd given nothing away, then. He'd thought she was speaking to Glen. Perhaps it was all for the best.

She worked at furious speed that afternoon to shut out all unwelcome thoughts. For another, she mustn't spin this out. She would just give herself a brief, poignant time with her father. Then she would go. It wasn't fair to Gareth to live under the same roof with him.

When she changed for dinner she chose an elegant trouser-suit of a grey that matched her eyes, but had flecks of sparkly blue and purple lurex in it. She examined herself closely in the mirror. She looked very drawn. Her cheeks were quite hollow. There were shadows under her eyes. They didn't look like the girl who'd been speaking to her betrothed half a world away. She ought to have been sparkling.

Gareth was astute—far too much so for his own peace of mind. Otherwise he'd never have guessed at first that she wasn't crazy about Glen. Meanwhile, eye-shadow would help this. Better for him to think she'd overdone her make-up than think she was fretting over something. A little colour too. She picked up violet eye-shadow. She added pendant earrings, amethyst ones Philippa had given her long ago. They had always done something to heighten her colouring.

Prudence looked at her over the big oval dish of lamb shanks she'd arranged on a bed of fluffy rice and red and green peppers, as she served out, piling a diced bacon barbecue sauce on top of each helping. 'You look very beautiful tonight, Faith. What lovely colouring that suit has! And those earrings are just perfect with it. I've always loved amethysts. With grey eyes they're no less than perfect. My sister Faith loved them too. You look quite partyish.'

Gareth took his plate from Prudence, said, 'And so she should! By rights it ought to be an engagement party! I can't think of anything more frustrating than getting engaged by phone, with all the Pacific and Atlantic Oceans in between, to say nothing of a continent or two, separating oneself and the loved one!'

The whole scene immediately riveted itself into a still-life study. Prudence's serving-spoon dropped rice and chopped peppers unheeded on the cloth. No one, in that first moment, looked delighted. Surprised, but not glad. In fact shocked would be a better description.

Then, as one, they rallied. Well, the women did. Robert remained as he was, just watching Faith. They said the usual things one does say in the first reaction to sudden news.

Prudence thought of something. 'Gareth, how come *you* knew? Why keep it to yourself till now? Surely we could have done something to help Faith celebrate! Lamb shanks! I could have got a turkey out of the freezer, and looked out some sparkling white wine. We've no champagne.'

Faith said, rather shakily, 'No need for champagne. I like this still rosé best. I——'

Gareth's voice was dry. That meant he was still angered. 'Oh, there'd have been no time to unfreeze a turkey, Gran. It happened only this afternoon. I happened to overhear the last of it when I came in to see how the three o'clock cuppa was progressing. They'd got to planning a honeymoon in the autumn in the Lake District and the Highlands, so there must have been some long preliminaries. Let's hope the poor bloke's got enough cash for a honeymoon by the time he's paid for that lot.'

Hope said, 'Where was he calling from, Faith?' Her voice was a little flat.

Faith swallowed. 'London.' It was all she could say.

Chassie's voice was also flat. 'You should have told us, dear. Nice to share news like that.'

Gareth said, 'Oh, Faith's a great one for keeping her own counsel. She knows all the family secrets, but we know none of hers. If I'd not overheard I doubt if she'd have told us.'

Prudence said a little sharply, 'Well, maybe she had her reasons. She's so considerate of other folks' feelings, she might have thought we'd get worried in case she took off for England before she finished the book.'

Gareth said, 'That never occurred to me. I had an idea that a chap who waited till he was the other side of world to pop the question, after knowing her for years, wouldn't exactly rush her off her feet. I'm sure Faith'll finish the book. She's not exactly being swept into matrimony.'

Even Robert looked startled at his tone. For a moment it looked as if he was going to reprove his step-grandson. But Faith had recovered and came in. 'Of course you didn't think of it. You heard me saying autumn. That's September–October in the British Isles. This is only June. I'm going to have the first three-quarters of that book into its final typing before your parents get here, and the rest ready for their additions. I wouldn't dream of turning this job in till it's ready for the printer.'

Prudence said gently, 'Glen must be staying there longer than he thought, Faith?'

'Yes. He may even take a position there. He first suggested that by letter. We can decide that after we're married.'

Oh, dear, she was certainly getting in deeply. Who was it had said a lie has no legs, it always needs another and another to prop it up? It would take only one person from Hawkes Bay who knew the Tankervilles to blow it sky-high. She hoped no one here had correspondents in Napier or Hastings! She knew the sickness of fear flutter her stomach. She subdued it, said, 'By the way, nothing is to be announced yet. It's a secret for the time being. It's awkward at a distance like this.'

Gareth seemed determined to be awkward. 'Oh, I don't know. You often see engagements announced from country to country. Till now I've thought it quite romantic. But perhaps you're not at all a romantic, Faith, when you're not writing!'

Robert said, 'Gareth! Stop baiting the lassie. I *will* not have it.' They all looked surprised. Robert added, 'I'm never in favour of sudden announcements. Rushing into print too soon has kept many a girl from backing out of a marriage she's not sure about. Now, would someone like to hand me the salt and pepper and stop discussing Faith's affairs!'

It was the only meal Faith could remember at Goblin Hill that hadn't been eaten in harmony. They were just finishing their apple tart when the phone went.

Gareth went to it. He said to the operator, 'What? Goodness, it's sure our day for international calls. This is the second.' Faith went hot, then cold. It could be Mark again. Something he'd forgotten to say. She half rose. Gareth waved her down. 'It's not for you. It's from Arizona. The folk must be getting nearer home ... I beg your pardon, Jess?' This was to the operator, a local girl. 'Oh, person-to-person for Mrs Robert Morland. Sure she's here. Just hang on.'

Prudence went across to the instrument, had to wait. The girl Jess must have said something to her. Prudence laughed, 'Yes, isn't it exciting? Even for our wee exchange ... one from London, one from Arizona, all in a matter of hours.'

Faith swallowed, coughed, choked, seized her glass, sipped hastily. Heaven send it wasn't the same operator as this afternoon. Prudence said, 'What did you say, Jess? Oh, was it? Who did you say? Fancy that. But that——' She broke off, 'Oh, is it coming now?' Then they heard her say, 'Oh, hullo, Leonie. This is lovely, so soon after your other call. I only hope you've got enough money left to get you home! But I mustn't waste time, what is it, love? Is Julian all right? Oh, good. No, I'll not let on to him by letter that you rang again. I love secrets —hope it's a nice one. Oh, I see. All right. Yes, they *are* here, goggling at me, listening to every word. I'll go to the other phone.'

She said, 'It's about the twins' birthday. Gareth, replace that receiver when I get round there, it echoes otherwise.' She hurried out.

Gareth stood with the phone in his hand, talked to his mother till he heard Prudence's voice at the other end.

Then he said, 'What a cheek you've got, Mama! Well, I am insulted! Don't see why I can't be in on what to get the twins in America. Well, bye-bye, take care of yourself and Dad.' He hung up. He came back to the table grinning. 'I wanted to share the conversation—didn't think the aunts' birthday presents would be top secret.'

It was Faith's turn to sound derisive. 'Poor Gareth! He thinks everyone should bare their inmost souls. He's almost got a complex about such things.'

They heard the phone in here tinkle as Prudence put the other one down, but she didn't come back right away. They heard her running upstairs. She seemed to be up there some time.

She looked a little strange when she came down. Faith told herself she was imagining that, but she caught Hope and Chassie exchanging puzzled looks. Robert said straight out, 'What's the matter?'

Prudence parried it. 'What do you mean? I said it was a secret.'

'I don't mean about the birthday, Prue. I mean you're out of breath and——'

Prudence managed an exasperated sigh. 'Of course I'm out of breath. At my age when I go upstairs I always am. I had to rummage round for something to make sure I told Leonie right. It was in one of the wardrobes in your room, Faith. Hope you don't mind. I just wanted to satisfy myself and get back before the rice gets too cold.'

'Mysteriouser and mysteriouser,' said Gareth. 'Well, here's your coffee, folks. I'll let you put in your milk yourself.'

'Oh, I'll just have mine black,' said Prudence. Odd ... she usually had it white. Faith saw Robert's eyes narrow as they rested on his wife. He wasn't a bit satisfied, she thought.

Oh, well, it was nothing to do with her. All that had happened today had simply underlined for her the fact that her stay here was very fleeting.

CHAPTER EIGHT

LIFE at Goblin Hill went on much the same on the surface. Faith typed hard and went for long, solitary walks over the downs and along the shore. Only when she rode did Gareth accompany her, so she seldom saddled up these days. That was because Robert allowed no one to ride round this craggy property alone, except the men. It dated from the night when that other Faith had lain injured and unconscious in the old quarry whence the blocks of stone for the homestead had been hewn, when her mount had thrown her after a stumble in a rabbit-hole. Harold had found her with an arm and a leg broken, and as a result of exposure her life had been despaired of for days.

Gareth had apparently overcome his first reaction to the part of the telephone conversation he'd overheard. His manner was casual, brotherly. The aunts and Prudence and Robert just wouldn't have tolerated a continuance of his manner that night. He went out more, to debating societies, to the Young Farmers' Club, political meetings, paid visits to neighbours. He didn't suggest Faith accompanied him.

He was outside a lot, clearing culverts, trimming willows, mending fences, did some early pruning in the garden. He even painted the fowlhouses. Glen still wrote. Perhaps Faith ought to have been glad of that, since it bolstered up her pretence. She curled her lip when in one Glen wrote, 'I am determined never to give up. Some day you'll realise it was no more than a lovers' tiff.'

Some day, said Faith to herself, I'll write and tell him I took only a small legacy from my mother. That what she didn't leave to Mark has gone to charities, to homes for unwanted children. It had been Philippa's reparation. That would put an end to it.

This day the older folk were over at the ranch-house giving it a springclean-in-winter against the Morlands' return. Faith went down for the mail, came back to tip them out on the kitchen table and fell with delight on one from Mark, two from friends in Napier, began to read them.

Gareth came in, said, 'Any coffee going? Oh, you've got the mail, good show. I was going to get it myself when I was up this end.' These days they had the coal range on from early morning onward. She pulled the singing kettle to the stove-lid over the fire-box, spooned the coffee powder into two mugs, put out some biscuits.

Gareth snapped the band off the big pile of magazines that had come. They were mostly farming ones. He said, 'There's an English one for you. They've sent it airmail.'

She glanced at it casually. 'Oh, yes, it's been forwarded from Napier. I suppose it contains a review of Dad's latest book. It would be out about that date. The complimentary copies will come by surface, of course, and they take about two months or more now there are so few ships. I'll take mine through with me. I've got a goal of so many pages today.' She avoided tête-à-têtes with Gareth these days.

She'd returned to her typing when the door flew open. She looked up as it banged back. What was the urgency? She saw signs of anger on Gareth's face and her heart sank. Had he, could he have found out her engagement was a fake?

He had the magazine with him. He flung it down on old Duncan's leather-topped desk. It was open at a spread of coloured photographs. 'I suppose you knew what was in this ... book review indeed.'

Faith looked. Her mother's exquisite features gazed up at her. So did Mark's. She gulped, said indignantly, 'How could I possibly know anyone would send me this? I'd no idea what was in that magazine! I'm pretty sure a book review of Dad's *will* be in it. If I'd known Philippa Meredith's photo was in it, I'd certainly never have left it out for you to see. Gareth, you really *have* got a complex about Philippa. These magazines will be in all the New Zealand shops in a few weeks. What on earth's it got to do with me?'

His lips were a thin line, his eyes scornful. 'Everything to do with you, I'd say! I suppose had I not seen this you'd never have told me you knew her, and intimately!'

Faith's heart hammered against her ribs. It was out, then. Some nosy journalist must have unearthed Philippa's secret and made copy from it. Gareth would say to hell with the family history and have her out of here tonight. Her mouth felt dry. The pictures wavered in front of her gaze as if she looked at them through water. Then they came into focus again.

Gareth's voice cut through the singing in her ears. 'You ought to have told me when I was singing my hymn of hate about her at our first meeting! I'd have had you out of here in double-quick time, believe me! Now you've wormed your way into everyone's affections. Look at that picture!'

It was one taken three years ago in that Haslemere garden, an autumn scene with the beeches incredibly golden, a carpet of leaves beneath the garden swing where Faith and Philippa were sitting. Lucy and Stephen Charteris were bending over one of Mark's Golden Labradors, Mark himself was leaning on a sundial.

Faith wore a sleeveless summer frock, all blues and purples; Philippa was in emerald green, her copper hair loosely tumbled round her shoulders. She looked so young, so vibrantly healthy, and now all that glowing vitality and talent were no more.

She kept the tears back by a tremendous effort. Gareth's forefinger was stabbing the page. 'Couldn't you have told me you were her goddaughter?'

Faith, who had risen to brace herself against complete

revelation of her identity, swayed a little, caught at her chair-back, steadied. Goddaughter! Not daughter. She rallied as he barked out, 'So you were named for *her*! Meredith Faith Charteris! Ye gods. What a nerve you had to come here at all!' Something struck him. 'Or—or was it possible you didn't know that the owner of Goblin Hill had been married to and deserted by Philippa Meredith?'

Faith sought for the right words.

He said, 'Come on, come on. Answer me, just this once, with truth, with no evasions. Must you always seek for words that are less than truth, Faith? If you didn't know. If it happened by sheer chance that my aunts saw your advertisement and wrote to you and you didn't know till I shot off my mouth, at our first meeting, about my hate of Philippa Meredith, I'll understand that you thought it best to say nothing. But for God's sake tell me the truth for once. Did you or didn't you know she'd been married to Dad when you applied for the job?'

Faith couldn't keep on lying. But she wouldn't tell all. That would be more hurtful still. She looked him straight in the eye. 'I knew before I came here.'

At the look on his face she would have caught the words back had she been able to. But words aren't homing pigeons. He'd hoped against hope she'd not known. He'd have understood her reticence had it been sheer coincidence she'd come here.

'Why, Faith? Why, oh, why? What brought you here? Sheer idle curiosity? How prying of you! You wanted to see what sort of a man your godmother had married first. How glad I am Dad was away. And you've pried into all our secrets. Perhaps writers are like that. They like to find out what makes us tick. They put human feelings under microscopes. Ohhhhh!' he gritted his teeth.

She felt helpless to explain, to excuse. She said stumblingly, 'I—I don't know what made me come. I felt a sort of compulsion. Philippa—my godmother—talked a lot to me about Goblin Head. I wanted to see it for myself.'

He looked bewildered. 'When did she talk to you about it?'

A look of desolation passed over her face. It moved him against his will. He took a step towards her, checked himself, as a man would who'd been made a fool of once and didn't want to have it happen again.

Faith said quietly, 'In the last few days before she died.'

He said, 'You were in England as recently as that?'

She nodded. 'Yes. Mark—her second husband and producer—wanted me there. I helped nurse her. You see, my father and mother were her closest friends. Mark asked me to stay till she went. He doesn't have anybody—just friends, not kin. He's a wonderful person. I love Mark more than anybody I've got left. I'd do anything for him.' She lifted her eyes from the carpet. She said, with a lift of the chin that had sheer courage in it had she but known, 'Gareth, we must take all people as we find them. To you, Philippa was the woman who brought your loved stepfather much unhappiness, the woman you thought your mother might fear. To me, and to my people, she was a loved and valued friend. No one rued more than she did what she'd done to your stepfather. I think she suffered remorse over it all her life. But she made what reparation she could.

'Not to him. But she had a great understanding of other people. I know of established actors and actresses of today who owe their first successes to her. She endowed a very gracious home in Devon where theatrical people who weren't a success could spend holidays in the country with their children between engagements. Her money is to go to the maintenance of foster-homes for children whose lives have been disrupted by either bereavement or marriage breakdown.'

He'd gone very quiet after his outburst, and was white under his tan. 'Oddly enough I can accept all that. I realise I've judged her solely on the actions of her thoughtless youth, but I don't think I could even begin to understand *your* motives in coming here.'

There was nothing she could do about that. The whole truth would hurt him even more because, though he might understand her craving to see where her ancestors had hewn out a living for themselves, it would give her the right to stay, and as it stood at the moment, he could banish her.

She said, 'What do you want me to do? I'll abide by whatever you decide.'

He walked to the study windows, stood looking across the leafless trees to the shore of Scimitar Bay. He turned round. They measured glances.

He said slowly, 'I don't want any emotional damage done to the aunts, or Gran and Grandy. I don't think they've ever taken any stranger to their hearts as they have you. It's odd. I'd like it to stay that way. Only you must shorten your time here.

'Someone's bound to see that magazine and remark on it. The girls will see it. The soonest it could get here would be six weeks. I want you gone before then. When you're out of it, it won't matter so much, your unpardonable curiosity. You've a good excuse. You can say Glen's put the wedding forward to suit the plans he's working on. But don't tell them yet. Get on with the book till it's at the stage where the last of it can be revised by me. Dad can add his bits, or work them in. You must be gone before they get home. Their arrival will just about coincide with the arrival of the magazine. I think my mother's had enough of Philippa Meredith in her life. I don't want her nosey goddaughter here.'

Faith moistened her lips. 'I think that's fair enough. I'll play it your way. Back me up when I announce that I'm going sooner. I don't want anyone to suspect till I'm gone. Can you cut down on your snide remarks like those you made when you heard me on the phone?'

'I'll discipline myself to that, but don't let it be too long.' He went out. A few minutes later she saw him on

Diogenes, riding towards the far boundary.

The others didn't seem to notice any undue acceleration in her pace on the typescript, beyond Prudence saying she was making good progress and what a good thing. She'd be able to be over the hills and far away when spring came.

Gareth grinned. 'Correction, Gran. She'll want to be on a plane and off on the wings of the wind to her beloved when the New Zealand spring comes. That's autumn in Britain. Good show. You must be nearly finished, Faith.'

Chassie said anxiously, 'But there's Julian's contribution yet. Leave space for it. Another month and they'll be home.'

Gareth's eyes met hers. She said to him late that night when the others had said goodnight, 'I'll be through in about ten days. Then I'll pretend Mark's run me and wants me over there sooner.'

Gareth said quickly, 'What do you mean, *Mark*? You mean Glen!'

She recovered herself. 'Of course I mean Glen. Did I really say Mark? Absentmindedness. I was writing to Mark today. He's back in London.'

'Where's he been?'

'In Hollywood, on business.'

'They get around, these bods, don't they?'

'They do. But travel loses its freshness when you have to do it so often. Mark's days are often longer than yours. Gareth, I'll have to have one or two sessions with you on the manuscript before I go, so you can consult with Julian on it. I've worked things out pretty well. Also, I've made a plan about my going. When they come back from visiting someone some day, I'll announce that I've had a ring from Glen, and say I immediately booked a place for the caravan on the roll-on, roll-off ferry across the Strait, so I can get it back to Napier. That I'll take off from Auckland as soon after that as possible. I'll see the publisher on the way and say he can send the proofs to you when your stepfather has added his stuff. I'll say I've to go to London urgently on business with Dad's publisher. He'll think nothing of that.'

'Why not say it's for a wedding? What better reason?'

Faith said, 'I've a very good reason for not broadcasting the wedding date yet. You can put it down to my secretive nature. And so it is. I've no intention of explaining it to anyone.'

Gareth shrugged, 'Please yourself. Goodnight,' and went to see all was locked up for the night.

That was Tuesday. On Thursday Faith was typing, but for the first time since she'd speeded up, she felt very weary of it. The joy had gone out of it. Every night she felt completely exhausted.

Prudence had said to her only last night, kissing her with the tenderness she'd have used had she indeed known she was kissing her own granddaughter goodnight, 'Faith dear, don't push yourself so hard. Surely time's not as precious as all that. It's only July.'

Faith had kissed her back. 'Oh, not to worry. Dad always got like this towards the end of a book. He started to race. I can understand him now. But I'll revive once it's done. Goodnight, Gran.'

She clapped her hands over her mouth. 'Oh, Mrs Morland, do forgive me! I must be catching it off Gareth.'

The pansy-brown eyes looked at her laughingly. 'I liked that, dear child. Life denied me grandchildren of my own, but I've been so fortunate to have step-grandchildren like Gareth, Megan and Rowena. I'd like to add you to them, because it's so sweet to have someone who bears my dead sister's name call me Gran.'

Faith put her arms about her, hid her face against the snowy hair with its faint hint of ripe gold, said, 'Oh, you are so winsome. You and Mr Morland have made me feel almost as if I belonged. Thank you for that. It's something I'll never forget.' As she put her cheek against the pink-and-white one of the woman who was in reality

148

her own flesh-and-blood, she was surprised to find it damp. Tear-damp. Oh well, she'd just mentioned Julian having no son to follow him. That would be it.

Now Faith shook herself free of the sweetness of that memory, slid another lot of pages and carbon into the typewriter, bashed on.

The door opened and she looked up. Who was this? A stranger. But a smiling stranger who didn't mutter: 'Oh, sorry, do excuse me.' Must be some relation to walk in unannounced like this. That would be it, because he reminded her of someone. Was it of Gareth? No, wrong colouring. He had silver hair, a young face, high cheekbones like Prudence's, a cleft chin ... grey eyes ...

He said, 'I believe the name is Faith ... guess who I am?'

Faith's eyes widened. She felt a joy like a warm spring tide rising within her. She came to her feet, knocked a pile of typescript off the desk, said, 'Oh, you're m——' she stopped just in time. She'd almost said, 'Oh, you're my father!' She managed to appear as if she'd tripped over her words and changed them to, 'You're Mr Morland. Julian Morland. I—knew you from your photograph.'

He stepped forward, said, 'I've heard so much about you I'm sure my wife'd let me kiss you ... doing a job like this for us, you're practically family.' He dropped a laughing kiss upon her cheek and she thought he'd never know how near she came to throwing her arms about him. Oh, but this was a little miracle! Ever since Gareth had ordered her early departure, she'd thought she'd never behold her father in the flesh, this man who had sired her.

There was a scurry and Leonie burst in. 'Isn't this just wonderful? I love giving people surprises. It looks as if your mother kept the secret well, Julian. Who says women can't keep them? She didn't dare tell Robert, or he'd have given it away for sure. She must have just about burst out with it at times. Faith, my dear, we're a mad family. You'll just have to take us as you find us. Greetings, sweetie.' She kissed Faith. 'Oh, Julian, just look at the poor girl, she's about overcome. She must wonder when the MacIntyre clan will come to an end. Though of course I'm just an offshoot-in-law. And I suppose bursting in like this has stopped the life-history dead in its tracks?'

Faith recovered, laughed, said, 'Nothing could do that, Mrs Morland. It's too vital. All the ingredients of a story were here from the time the earliest MacIntyre turned the first sod. It must have lain in the very natures of that young couple. They had what it takes, and that courage and vitality have lasted right through the years.'

Leonie nodded. 'Generation after generation, and each with problems of their own ... who's to say which one surmounted most? But they were tough and resilient and fun-loving, like the aunts and Julian's parents.' She sighed. 'Above everything else, I wish it didn't have to end there. I'd have liked someone with MacIntyre blood to carry on for Julian.'

Julian said quickly, 'But my wife's son will carry on. If I'd had a son he mightn't have wanted to be a farmer. So I know no regrets.' The look he gave Leonie was satisfying, tender.

Leonie said, 'But the regrets are mine. If only you'd had a daughter, even. After all, your mother was the daughter of the last MacIntyre son, and produced you.'

Faith found she was clenching her teeth. Julian gave a short, almost embarrassed laugh. 'What a subject to bring up in front of Faith, five minutes after we've first met!'

Leonie looked demure. 'Didn't you once tell me, when you proposed so precipitately, that time was relative when it came to recognising kinship of spirit?'

Julian slapped her. 'I've never known anyone so given to tripping a man up with his own words!' He grinned at Faith, 'But she's right. You can't be a stranger when you know all our secrets. And the family have written reams about you, even Gareth. I thought they were all imagining the likeness to Aunt Faith, but they're right. You're just like her photograph. Pity it hadn't been a coloured one, it would have been even more striking. I'm told I've the same colouring.'

Leonie looked from one to the other, consideringly. She had an odd look on her face. 'You certainly have,' she said. For a moment Faith felt uneasy. How terrible for Gareth if, at this late moment, Leonie tumbled to something the others would never have dreamed of. But that was absurd. Why should anyone entertain so wild a surmise? They thought of her as a well-known author's daughter. And she would be gone from here long before that wretched magazine came to these shores to link her in any way with Philippa. She could imagine Gareth's wrath if anything set off suspicion.

Leonie said, 'What a pity you have to leave so soon. Not that you'll think that way when you're leaving to be married, but we'd have loved you to have been still in New Zealand when the book's published. We thought we'd have a sort of celebration, a district one. Perhaps an old-time dinner and dance in the woolshed.'

Faith was finding this painful. Leonie was so like Gareth, the warm brown eyes, not dark, more the colour of dry sherry. Tawny brows that in her case were groomed into smooth wings. Tawny-brown hair that curved round her face and clustered round neck and jawline in petalled strands. She looked so girlish to be Gareth's mother ... until you noticed the lines of discipline around that sweet mouth. But there was no bitterness as there might have been. Faith had an idea that happiness had so crowned this woman's later years, she was conscious always of gratitude. No wonder Prudence loved her daughter-in-law. Suddenly Faith knew it was right she should leave here soon, should leave this happiness undisturbed. Meanwhile, the earlier return of her father was an unexpected bonus.

She said, putting the cover on the typewriter, 'Well, I

couldn't settle to any more typing today. I'll come out and get on with the dinner so the others can talk to you to their hearts' content.'

Leonie laughed. 'The dinner's under way. Julian's mother knew, as I said. She'd secretly stuffed a turkey and has it in the oven with all the trimmings. She's made Julian's favourite pudding, apple amber. Have you had it yet, Faith?'

'No, it sounds gorgeous.'

'It is. She sets spirals of apple slices all round the bottom of a pudding bowl in brown sugar and butter. Then she pours in a sponge mixture with spices added, and steams it. When she turns it out the design is beautiful, with the apple crescents set in a sort of butterscotch caramel.'

'That really sets my taste-buds going,' said Julian, shepherding them out of the room, an arm round their shoulders. 'I only hope to goodness it's not far off ... ah, I hear crashing footsteps approaching. It can only be Gareth.'

Faith felt butterflies in her stomach. He was going to be furious she was still here. She slipped behind the Morlands. Gareth lifted his mother clean off her feet, kissed her, turned to hug his stepfather.

Faith managed to corner him in the bathroom before the meal. She saw him go in, tapped, said, 'Gareth, may I speak to you?'

He let her in. She said breathlessly, 'I'm sorry about this. But please don't worry over it. Don't let anything take from you the joy of having your parents back home. I'll be gone long before that magazine reaches here.'

She couldn't read his expression. He stood there, holding the dripping soap over the basin, considering it. Then, surprisingly, he said, 'Don't hurry your going any more. You've given Gran and Grandy an approximate date. Leave it at that.'

'You mean in case it sets them wondering?'

'Not really. Somehow, with Mother home, I feel a little

more confident that we can—that we can carry things off without any harm being done. I don't know why, but she has that effect on me.'

'Not only on you. I felt it immediately. I felt terrible at first, but then I lost my fear. I wonder what it is, that quality. No wonder Mr Morland looks so happy, so young.'

Gareth smiled a little. 'Yes, he said once, giving me advice on marriage—Oh, just in a general way—to pick a life-partner with great care. Said he'd like to see me with someone like my mother, and added, "Because she has the power to turn water into wine."'

Faith's eyes lit up. 'Oh, that's tremendous. It sums her up. I'll find your dad very stimulating if he can produce thumbnail sketches like that.' The brown eyes met the grey. Both pairs looked swiftly away. Faith said hurriedly, 'I must go. That turkey's nearly ready to be carved.'

She rushed out of the bathroom and collided with Robert. He steadied her. 'Lass, do you need to come out of doors like a whirlwind?'

'Sorry, Robert, I don't want to hold dinner up.' She clapped her hands over her mouth. 'I mean, Mr Morland.'

Her grandfather grinned at her. 'At my age you appreciate someone thinking of you that way.' He put out a hand to the bathroom door.

Faith said, 'There's someone in there. Gareth.' She felt awkward. But old Robert only said, 'Oh aye, is there now? Well, we really are like one family, when you can even share a bathroom. I'll away down to the one off the kitchen.' He chuckled as he went.

She sat between her grandfather and grandmother at the meal. Robert said, helping himself to cranberry jelly, 'This girl gave me the thrill of my life. She called me Robert. When you get to my age, it's something to think one of the younger lot thinks of you as Robert Morland, as a person, not just someone's father or grandfather, much and all as I appreciate Gareth calling me that seeing I've no descendants of my own.'

Faith noticed an interchange of looks between Prudence and Leonie. What was it? Sympathy? They both knew a yearning, it seemed. Because of the estate.

She said quickly, 'Of course, having written up the history, from your childhood days, I think of you by your Christian names. And not just you. I think of Duncan and Euphemia and Olivia and James, that way too, and Faith.'

Prudence said, 'I stopped off at the church yesterday to fill up the vases and I found fresh flowers on all the graves. Early violets and primroses. Was it you, Faith?'

She crimsoned. 'Yes, I——'

'Dear, don't look so embarrassed. I thought it was lovely. I know they'll never be forgotten.'

What a strange thing to say when Prudence knew she'd be half a world away very soon.

Prudence continued, 'I can't think where you got so many. Even by that sheltered wall in the garden there are so few. Unless you——' she looked a question.

Faith nodded. 'I remembered you telling me that your sister Faith planted a garden round your old tree-house in the Hansel-and-Gretel Wood by the shore. I went down to see it so I could describe it in the book. In the part where I bring in the things that have lingered on into the present day, and it's just carpeted with violets and primroses.'

Robert nodded. 'It always is. It makes me feel as if the very earth remembers Faith.'

Faith said, 'Oh, another lovely phrase! What a day this has been! I'll use that.'

Julian said interestedly, 'What was the other?'

Faith said, 'Er——' and stopped.

Gareth said hastily, 'It was just something I told her.'

Leonie looked saucy. 'Such as what? Do share it, son. Oh, you're blushing too! Sorry, son. Forget I asked.'

Gareth said still more hastily as Robert began to chuckle, 'I was just repeating a phrase you used once,

Dad. About Mother. No, I'm not going to repeat it. It wasn't for general chit-chat.'

Robert said deliberately, 'No, I expect not, and you certainly had all the privacy you wanted, didn't you, in the bathroom.'

Faith and Gareth looked embarrassed again. Then Faith said, 'Look, I just wanted to ask Gareth something before dinner, saw him going in and slipped in for the moment. Robert, you're being very naughty, it wasn't an assignation. Sorry about that, Gareth, it was a bit stupid of me.' She looked at them all severely. 'It may sound interesting, I mean about the phrases, but all these things are grist to a writer's mill.'

'Besides which,' said Gareth, 'if we repeated it, my lady mother would get a swelled head, and she's cock-a-hoop enough already. Must be the effect of getting home.'

He got up. 'Faith and I will wash the dishes and let you get on with the chatting. We'll bring in the coffee after.'

When they heard the news coming on on the television, Faith said, 'In some way see if you can stop them looking at *The Pengarths* tonight. I mean, perhaps you could say, switching off, "Well, we've got more interesting things to talk about tonight." I think it would be wise!'

Gareth said, 'Thanks for suggesting that. But I've thought over what you said about Philippa being a loved and valued friend to your family. I do realise we each have to take people as we find them. I'll never, of course, understand why you came here. I can't help regarding that as an unwarranted intrusion. But you've done a great job for my family. I respect your loyalty to your godmother, and as you loved her so much I don't feel I've any right to deprive you of watching any instalment.'

Faith couldn't speak for a moment. She scrubbed furiously at the perfectly clean sink, then said, 'Thanks, Gareth, I appreciate that. It's more than I deserve. But for your mother's sake, if you can dodge having it on, do.'

Other people had the same idea. As they brought in

the coffee, the local news finished and Hope got up and switched off. 'We're certainly not going to waste time on TV tonight. There are better things to do.'

Leonie said, 'Well, I don't care about the other programmes, but we'll certainly have *The Pengarths* on at quarter to eight. We missed so much of it travelling. Everywhere we went they were at a different sequence, though we caught up with some when we were staying with friends in the States. From what the girls said when we called up at the school, since you've had three sessions a week the last few months, you're almost up to where it was there.'

Nobody spoke. She added, 'I never did mind it, you know, and since I met Philippa in the flesh, and Mark Denby too, I'm even keener. They took us up to the studios, you know, and we met the whole cast. I'm only sorry there'll be an end to it. I believe they've done it beautifully, though. Philippa herself suggested the ending. I've heard it seems almost impossible to believe she isn't the grandmother she appears to be, they made her up so well. She's supposed to die at sunset on the very day her first grandchild is put into her arms and says, "Something I thought I'd never see ... another Pengarth to carry on".'

Faith got such a surprise she said, 'But who told you? Has it leaked, after all?' Then a moment later, realising she'd got carried away, she said, 'I saw something—in the paper—About it being a well-guarded secret. I——'

Leonie said, 'Oh, we ran into Mark Denby in Los Angeles. I believe it was to be a secret at first, but he said it was out now.'

Faith was sure Gareth leaned forward in his chair to shield her a little from their sight. He said, 'Los Angeles? I thought you said in your letters you were going to fly from Vancouver. Said you'd seen Los Angeles on the way over.'

Julian said, 'We changed our plans. Having decided it would be nice to be back for the twins' birthday and wanting to visit the Claymores in Idaho, and the Butes in Arizona, we decided to continue on. We were glad we did when we met Mark. We saw him in Toronto too, but that wasn't by chance, we knew he was going to be there. He's looking thinner, but he's so busy I think it's been the saving of him. A grand chap.'

Faith was glad Gareth was still leaning forward. Mark had kept quiet about seeing them in Canada. Why?

Leonie said, 'Mark was so different from my idea of a film tycoon, so ordinary ... except on the set. He said Philippa was magnificent to the last. She was quite well, outwardly, when we were there. I'm glad we met. Mark said to us in L.A. that it had made it a lot easier for her, seeing us together, knowing Julian was happy.' Faith had an idea she was speaking at Gareth, if not directly to him. 'She and I had a talk on so much I don't feel I've any right to deprive you of watching any instalment.'

Faith couldn't speak for a moment. She scrubbed furiously at the perfectly clean sink, then said, 'Thanks, Gareth, I appreciate that. It's more than I deserve. But for your mother's sake, if you can dodge having it on, do.'

Other people had the same idea. As they brought in the coffee, the local news finished and Hope got up and switched off. 'We're certainly not going to waste time on TV tonight. There are better things to do.'

Leonie said, 'Well, I don't care about the other programmes, but we'll certainly have *The Pengarths* on at quarter to eight. We missed so much of it travelling. Everywhere we went they were at a different sequence, though we caught up with some when we were staying with friends in the States. From what the girls said when we called up at the school, since you've had three sessions a week the last few months, you're almost up to where it was there.'

Nobody spoke. She added, 'I never did mind it, you know, and since I met Philippa in the flesh, and Mark Denby too, I'm even keener. They took us up to the studios, you know, and we met the whole cast. I'm only sorry there'll be an end to it. I believe they've done it beautifully, though. Philippa herself suggested the ending. I've heard it seems almost impossible to believe she isn't the grandmother she appears to be, they made her up so well. She's supposed to die at sunset on the very day her first grandchild is put into her arms and says, "Something I thought I'd never see ... another Pengarth our own, in the garden. Julian and Mark had gone fishing. She'd carried a big burden of remorse all her life. I said to her we'd both paid dearly for the mistakes we'd made when we were young and foolish.'

Gareth stirred. 'It was a bit different, Mother.'

'Not so very different. We both made an error of judgment. Philippa knew she ought not to marry someone tied to the land when she had all this burning ambition. I had plenty of warnings of the instability of your father's character and married him in the face of all the advice of wiser people, just to gratify my own feelings. In so doing I brought much trouble on my children. On you more than your sisters, Gareth, because they were so much younger. Oh, I know all about remorse too. I told Philippa that. I can't tell you what it did to me, that experience. And it sort of tidied up all our lives.'

Faith knew Leonie had paid her the greatest compliment she could have, by speaking so openly like this in front of her. Prudence must have told her Faith knew about it.

So Leonie thought the past had been all tidied up. She thought his mother had even convinced Gareth now that it no longer mattered. And when Faith was gone from here and the series was over, there would be an end to it. The New Year would bring a happier era to Goblin Hill.

CHAPTER NINE

JULIAN spent almost as much time at the homestead as he did at the ranch-house. He was glad it was this time of year and that Gareth and John could manage the outside work with a bit of help from Robert.

'Gareth says they've done without me so long I can take all the time I like to work with you on the manuscript, Faith.'

Faith knew Gareth wanted no hold-up there. He was going to say when, eventually, that article in the magazine came to their notice, that she'd asked him not to reveal that she was Philippa's goddaughter. He'd added, 'I'm afraid your image will suffer. But it won't matter so much with you at the other side of the world.'

She knew she'd stay over there now. She could live with her stepfather and his sister. Mark could get her a job typing scenarios or something. She would never again see the sea beating up against South Cliffs, look out of her Aunt Faith's window to see that somnolent goblin lying on his back on the headland above the three houses on the estate ... never again linger beside the graves of her forebears, look at the memorial tablets in the little Puketaipo church for those who were buried in a distant continent. Never again to go riding with her grandmother and grandfather to the boundaries of the estate, have them point out historical spots, have them kiss her goodnight.

Worst of all, she'd never again see Gareth riding by on Diogenes, rider and horse carved as one against a blue winter sky ... never see Gareth humouring the great-aunts, never know the joy it would have given Hope and Chassie and Prudence and Robert to know that the Faith who occupied that other Faith's bedroom was indeed flesh of their flesh, bone of their bone. As for her father ... she counted every hour spent with him in the study as beads on a rosary to be counted over and over in memory in the years ahead.

There came the day when she knew the task was almost ended. While Julian had written out his notes for the later years she'd caught up on most of the re-typing of the earlier chronicles. Now his work had to be revised, brought into chronological order, and typed, and some sort of final chapter must be written.

Leonie said she had an inspiration about that. 'Faith, when you've got Julian's contribution typed, I have a feeling that once you get away from it piecemeal and read it as a coherent whole, the last chapter will suggest itself. How about doing just that?'

Faith thought it a good idea. Leonie said, 'Then I'll leave you to it,' and went out of the study. At the door she looked back at them, smiling.

'She looks just like the cat that's licked up the last of the cream,' said Julian uneasily. 'I don't trust my wife when she wears that expression. I wonder what she's up to.'

Faith smiled at him. 'Julian, I wouldn't worry. Anything Leonie ever does will be for someone's good.'

He put his hand over hers as it lay on her great-great-grandfather's desk, patted it, said, 'That's true. Thank you, Faith.' Then he looked doubtful. 'I think it's ultimately true, but the process is sometimes frightening. The rest of us go carefully round corners, Leonie cuts them.'

Faith looked at him. 'Sounds as if there might be some very interesting anecdotes left untold.'

'I'll say, but we've more than enough now.' He leaned his chin on his hand, said, 'There's something about you, Faith, that makes us want to keep telling you things, things we'd normally tell no one outside the family. Though even I was surprised when Leonie talked so freely in front of you that night we arrived home. About my first wife, I mean. It was a great compliment to you.'

Hadn't he realised it was Gareth Leonie had been getting at?

He turned his head, studying her a little. It made Faith a bit nervous. There was a likeness, she knew. He said, 'I wish you hadn't been leaving us. Pity. You know, perhaps I oughtn't to be telling you this, but we had great hopes that you and Gareth might have made a match of it. I mean, from the letters we got when you arrived. Not just the women, but even from Dad. Nothing would have delighted Leonie and myself more. We thought at first that the way they identified you with my Aunt Faith was wishful thinking. But it's true. Oh, well, likenesses crop up in the most unexpected places. But it's so strange, there's another resemblance that tantalises me now and then. It's your laugh. I just can't quite pin it down.'

Faith went very still. It was her mother's laugh. Before she could change the subject he added, 'I'm certain to track it down one of these days. By the way, before you go, we'd like to give you a wedding present. What would you like? Do tell us. Do you think you and Glen will come back to New Zealand, or stay over there? Because breakables are tricky.'

Faith knew panic. She said quickly, 'It's all so much up in the air at the moment, I couldn't say. I think we'll only decide after I get there. I'm not at the stage of thinking about wedding presents.'

He accepted that, picked up the morning paper and retired to an easy chair. 'Good heavens, that's getting a bit close to home! Mutton-poachers in the Shag Valley now. We've never suffered from it, but it's not to say we never will. They're cunning hounds. They remove all traces of the killings, so it can be weeks before a farmer realises his flock's getting down. I'd like to have a go with them. It's bad enough losing sheep to dogs, but you can usually put a stop to that. Trouble is, of course, they're off to another area before it's found out. In our size paddocks you're at their mercy. I think we'll start moving some of ours away from the paddocks that border on the road. They can't transport them so easily from inner paddocks. Flaming nuisance!'

Hope complained that Leonie wasn't over so much. 'After all that springcleaning we did at Lilac Bend, you wouldn't think she'd be so busy.'

Julian grinned. 'It's not the house she's busy on, she's having fun. A surprise for everyone. I'm not in on it yet. She's scribbling away like mad, and every now and then she laughs to herself. I think it's for the book. I've an uneasy suspicion she might have remembered something we'd rather was forgotten. However, I must abide my patience, as my grandfather used to say.'

Faith's eyes looked starry. His grandmother had been Olivia. She said, 'I just love it when D—— when Julian talks about Olivia.' She felt ill. Heaven send she never called him Dad outright! 'Julian, was she as beautiful as your mother and Hope and Chassie say? How did she appear to you?'

'She had the loveliest voice, Faith, singing and speaking. A contralto voice like yours. She'd tell me stories in the half-light. I went to sleep once and woke again. She was still by my bed. The last light of the sunset was just touching her hair. It was that strange dark-gold. I thought she was just like a painting. Odd for a little boy of about seven to think. I wish some artist could have painted her at that moment.'

Faith slipped away to insert that. It would mean three pages would have to be typed over, but that little boy's picture of his grandmother must go in, and when she recorded his wish she would put, 'But to live on in the hearts of those who loved us is the finest portrait of them all.'

Julian and Leonie didn't have dinner at the homestead that night. They had things to do at home. Leonie looked a little excited. Why? But at nine Julian poked his head round the door to say, 'Could you spare me an hour or so, son? John's out with Mattie tonight and I want a bit of help up home. And Faith, I've thought of something for the book if you'd come out here.'

The others continued to look at the news. Julian didn't lead them to the study, he took them into the kitchen. 'Gareth, I'm pretty sure we've got the mutton-poachers in. I went upstairs to the boxroom for something and happened to see torches flashing over at Quarry Gap. They're at the wethers. They know what they're doing all right. That's the only paddock with sheep in close to the road. We'll try not to disturb the dogs, though I guess that wouldn't worry the thieves—they'd know they were tied up this time of night.

'We dare not take the Land Rover, they'd hear us coming. Now, I don't want Dad out. You know what a goer he is when he gets his dander up. He'd get into a rough-house right away. I didn't ring the police from home because I couldn't be sure, but I went up the stable-loft over here and that's it for sure. So, Faith, would you ring the police from the study phone? If the others hear the click, you can say you rang Leonie about something. We may just lie and watch till they get here, but if they start to move off, we'll have to delay them. If we could see their truck number, it would be best of all. See you soon, we hope.'

Faith wasted no time, gave the exact locality and detailed instructions on which roads to take. But it would be at least half an hour before the police got here. She found she was shaking and her imagination ran riot. She'd a fair idea Julian and Gareth would welcome any chance to get into action. They'd taken pick-handles with them. Those men would have knives with them for the slaughtering! She couldn't stand it, she was going too. She'd keep back. With luck they might never know she'd disobeyed. But she'd be there, if anything went wrong. Though what help she'd be, she couldn't imagine.

She stuck her head in the door, said to the family,

'I'm going to Lilac Bend too,' and was away. She donned an anorak against the cold, but left the hood down so she could hear more clearly.

The ground was already shining white with frost and a pale moon was riding high. She wished the surf didn't pound so heavily against the cliffs. It was quite a distance, through several paddocks, but by now she was adept at mounting barbed-wire fences as Gareth. Twice as she breasted the rises she caught sight of the dark figures of her father and Gareth well ahead of her. They were keeping to the shadows as much as possible too.

In this light she could distinguish the outline of the hill above Quarry Gap, and once she caught sight of a flashing torch. Suddenly she had an idea. If she made straight across in the direction of the road, she might see the truck. If they were working from the Gap, it would be logical to have the vehicle this side, facing south because there was no exit the other way. She reached the gorse hedge by the road. Now go canny, Faith, don't step on any dry gorse. They could be dragging a couple of carcases along at any moment.

She had to negotiate another hedge that joined this at right angles. Not many gaps in this one. She crawled under where a tiny muddy stream hollowed it out. Oh, but the water was cold! Apart from that she was hot, sticky with apprehension on the men's behalf ... and scared for herself too. She saw the flash of a light, and voices frighteningly near at hand. Her flesh crept, came out in goose-pimples. She stopped dead, held her breath.

'What a weight!' said a voice. 'How many's that? Sixteen?'

Fury rose up in Faith, swamping fear. Those were her father's wethers! She heard them going away. They weren't exercising great caution. Must think they were too far away to need stealth.

An idea hit Faith. The truck was just there. She could not only get the number, but she could let the tyres down. Then they'd have to be here when the police arrived. Blast this hedge, it was so dense. But she dared not wait. She pulled the anorak over her face as far as possible and pushed through the thinnest place.

It was much harder to let tyres down than she thought. Her hands were stiff with cold, and these were brutes of things. It was a very large lorry. And she had to keep stopping to listen intently for sounds of a return. She'd just got one starting to go down when she heard them, much sooner than she'd hoped. They must have put other carcases over the hedge on to the road verge and were picking them up from there, not from the paddock.

She stole off to where Benjie's blasted oak marked a boundary between two paddocks, and lay down in the shadow. She just hoped that tyre stopped hissing before they got here, or that they made too much noise to notice it.

With great relief she heard them move off again. She strained her eyes in an endeavour to see how far they went. Then she heard sounds of creaking fence wires and knew they were going back to the scene of slaughter. Well, they weren't going to get away with it! She had the number committed to memory, though if it was a stolen truck, that wouldn't be traceable, but they'd be slowed up with what they'd think was a puncture and sheer bad luck. But if they suspected, they'd drive hell-for-leather on the rim to get away.

Then the idea hit her. Gravel in the petrol tank! Oh, please don't let it be a locking-cap. It wasn't. She clutched up handfuls of gravel and bunged it in, then screwed the cap back on. Shaking hands didn't help, but she managed it. She took a look on the cargo at the back of the truck and shuddered. Abattoir killing was humane, but this was butchery.

Just as she turned away pandemonium broke out. Yells rent the air, shouts, curses, thumps ... Gareth and Julian were in action!

Faith took a dive clean through the gap she'd made, minus any protection this time, and took off across the paddocks in a straight line. She went like the wind, quite unable to make out what was happening. All she wanted to do was get there. She heard a cry of pain she knew instantly was Julian's. If he was down, or injured, it would be Gareth against the lot. From what she'd heard, she guessed there were at least two more. Oh, how soon would the police be here? She didn't care now if the men got away before they arrived, they couldn't get far. As long as her two men weren't badly injured before that!

She shouted at the top of her voice, 'Help's coming. Help's coming! The police are nearly here. The police are coming!'

She didn't care if Gareth and Julian were furious with her. She only wanted to stop the fight before any harm was done to them. She heard cries and grunts of pain as thumps indicated contact and prayed her men weren't on the receiving end. Then there was a crashing that indicated one thing ... retreat through hedges ... thank God! Because those men had knives, freshly gory from their honourable work. She heard her slacks rip as she almost leapt the last fence, steadying herself by the post, then she rushed diagonally to the corner by the road.

She saw a burly figure, followed by two others, in full retreat along the road verge, then had a heart-stopping moment as she saw three forms on the ground, quite still. She went down by the first one. Julian! By the light of the moon she could see a nasty gash across his forehead. But he moved. She said, 'Dad, Dad, are you all right? Are you all right?' His eyes were closed. Only his hands moved. She groaned out loud.

It must have penetrated, he said, weakly, 'Gareth ... he's out to it. Go to him.'

She flew over to Gareth. No blood that she could see. His pick-handle lay beside him. She dropped to her knees, crying, though hardly aware she did, 'Gareth, Gareth, speak, speak! Oh, my darling, my darling. Oh, Faith, shut up, you fool! Feel his pulse ... his heart!'

Her stern strictures to herself steadied her. She pushed

her hand inside his jacket, felt his heart beating quite strongly, said, 'Thank God!'

At that moment her father shouted a warning, 'Faith, look out! Go for your life. Get help ... that chap's getting up.'

She spun round, seized the pick-handle, advanced on the man. He was on one elbow. Groggy, but dangerous, she knew.

She said, 'Lie down, you, and keep lying down, or I'll clobber you with this!' She brandished the pick threateningly. The fellow knew she meant business. He dropped down immediately, said, 'No, lady, don't. Don't! I've had it, I can't do you any damage.'

'You certainly have had it. I don't care what I do. If you'd killed either of them, I'd have laid you out with this without caring a jot! You'd better start praying they aren't seriously hurt. The police are on their way.'

Julian sat up, a hand to his face. 'Faith! Give me that pick-handle. I'm feeling better. And get right back to the house. This is too dangerous. Did you give the police clear directions?'

'I did, but they'll be delayed on their way stopping the truck. Julian, can you guard this chap while I attend to Gareth? I'm not leaving, so you can save your breath.'

'All right. Give it here.' He raised himself up painfully. 'I'm okay. I was only out to it temporarily. This chap tripped me up and I fell on to a rock. But I clobbered him as I fell. For goodness' sake look to Gareth.' He glared down at the man. 'And if you've seriously injured my son, God help you! And don't have any ideas about trying to get away, mate. As you can see, even the females of my family are pretty deadly.'

'I'll say!' muttered the man.

Faith knelt beside Gareth. At sight of his ominous stillness a sob escaped her. As she bent closer to peer at him, his lips moved and his eyes opened. 'Not to worry, Faith. I'm all right, but how's Dad? And what's going on?'

'Don't sit up. You don't know what injuries you may have. Your dad's all right, more or less.'

He turned his head. 'Ah, we got one of them. That's good, hope he splits on the others and they get the lot. But I'd have liked to have stopped the lot. Let me sit up, girl.'

'Not on your life! Just——'

Noises reached them, of an engine in trouble, and curses. Faith giggled. Julian said sharply, 'Faith, stop that. Don't get all hysterical on us. Stop it this moment, do you hear?'

She said, laughing helplessly, but trying to sound indignant, 'I'm not—hysterical, I mean. It's just that it's so funny. They're trying to start a truck that's got a petrol tank full of gravel and grass. And they've got a flat. I let the air out.'

A string of blue curses rent the air from the recumbent one. He started up as if to try to get away. Julian cracked him smartly on the shoulder. 'The next'll be on your head, mate, so be warned.'

Julian got up. He looked south, saw lights. 'Police cars for sure. So even if the men scatter now, they'll be rounded up with very little trouble. There's only the railway-line and the shore. They could cordon that off with no difficulty.'

Gareth said faintly, 'You ... let the tyre down? You filled the tank up with gravel? Oh, Faith, Faith, did you never think they might have caught you at it?'

'I should say I did! I was terrified. My knees were knocking. But luck was with me. I lay under Benjie's blasted oak when they came back once, then finished it after. But oh, if only I could have reached you before you attacked them, and told you, it'd have been more effective.'

Gareth said, 'Ah ... listen to that? Ever hear a more beautiful sound? Police sirens. They didn't use them till they were dead sure they were blocking the exit, I suppose.' He added 'ouch!' as he sat up, and put his hand to his head. 'I'm afraid I really did stop a whale of a clout.'

Faith made an exclamation. 'Where is it sorest? Oh, keep still, Gareth, that's blood dripping out of your sleeve. No wonder you went out to it. It's been bleeding all this time. Back you go.'

Julian, from his post, said, 'Can you manage, Faith? I've got a scarf on. Is it a deep cut?'

She managed to get his coat off and roll up his jersey and shirt sleeve. It was his upper arm, on the under side. A horrible gash.

'I saw the knife flash,' said Gareth, 'and put up my arm to save my face.'

Julian said quietly, 'You put your arm up to defend *my* face, then you copped it yourself and the other fellow bashed you on the head with a log.'

Faith said, 'Julian, I'll have to have help. I must stop this bleeding.'

Julian said savagely to the man he was guarding, 'Perhaps I ought to lay you out now so you can't make a move, but if you do while I'm attending to my son, God help you. In fact, I'll drag you over nearer.'

He did. Faith couldn't assist because she was pressing her handkerchief on to the wound as hard as she could.

Julian took out his handkerchief, rolled it into a hard pad, pressed it on top of hers, while she wound the scarf round as tightly as she could. She glared at their prisoner. 'If he gets infection in that, I just hope you get a maximum sentence!'

Gareth felt much better when the bleeding stopped. It was maddening hearing it all at a distance, but they had to stay where they were. It was the best moment of all when uniforms apeared over the fence, bent to their assistance. One of their number, expert in first-aid, bound Gareth's arm up in much more hygienic fashion; explanations flowed, one and all looked at Faith in a most approving fashion, though they were very grateful to Julian and Gareth too, apart from saying it might have been wiser to have waited. They'd got all the men.

They were put into a police car and taken round to the homestead. The look on the faces round the hearthside as they walked in reduced them all to laughter. The others simply boggled, as well they might. While they'd been peaceably watching a British crime film, members of their household had been bringing law-breakers here to justice.

'Well, Faith has,' said Gareth. 'Dad and I copped it very early in the piece, but she let down the tyre of the getaway truck and filled their tank with gravel and grass ...'

Faith said, 'That was nothing. Not like hand-to-hand conflict like you were. And you accounted for one, anyway. It was just that you were outnumbered, or you'd have brought the lot down.'

Julian chuckled. 'Well, I reckon you'd have engaged in the fighting given half a chance! That chap certainly thought you were going to clobber him. You acted in the true MacIntyre spirit.'

If only he'd known how true that was, thought Faith. She said crisply, 'Well, enough bouquets. The doctor from Palmerston should be arriving soon—the police got in touch by radio. I'd like to see these two washed up before he arrives. Julian had a very nasty crack when he fell on to that rock. He was out to it when I got there. That cut on his face needs attention too. Chassie, would you ring Leonie and tell her, without alarming her unduly, what's happened? She may have heard the screeching of cars, sirens and whatnot. Unless she had TV on full bore. It seems none of you heard it.'

Julian said, 'John Bruce will be hopping mad he missed all this by being at that party in Dunback.'

Faith sighed. 'That's the difference between the sexes. Now me, I'd have been very glad to have missed it.'

Julian said, 'How odd, at one stage I'd the feeling you were thoroughly enjoying it. That young constable thought so too. He said to Gareth, "Who's she? Has she ever thought about joining the Force?"'

Gareth lifted his head from the couch. 'To which I replied, "You're of of luck, mate. She's getting married before Christmas. In England."'

It set Faith back, made her remember her position. One moment she was one of the family, the next just someone who'd helped them compile the history, someone whom one member would be glad to see depart from Goblin Hill.

Gareth went on chuckling. 'Mind you, I think if he'd heard her just before they arrived, it would have spoiled her image. She suddenly felt sorry for that chap, went across to him and said, "Do you have a wife and children? You do? Then don't you think it would be less tough on them if you worked for your living instead of getting in with a gang like this?" It really took that fellow aback. He finally said, "Well, thanks, lady. You could be right." We'd better not tell Mother that or she'll be bent on carrying on the work of reforming him and we'll find ourselves visiting him in prison.'

'Why not?' said Prudence. The men groaned. To change the subject of future attempts at this, Faith said, 'Well, I expect I was just trying to restore my own image of myself. Wasn't I bloodthirsty? I felt I could really understand Boadicea for the first time. You've only got to see those you love injured, for you to feel really warlike.' It was just as well she didn't see some of them exchanging glances.

The doctor arrived, stitched Gareth's arm, gave him an injection against infection, dressed the wound on Julian's face, and examined his head. No cause for anxiety, he thought, but advised them to have a quiet day tomorrow.

Leonie and Julian stayed down at the homestead overnight.

Faith herself slept like a top with no need of the sedatives the doctor had prescribed for the two men, to their disgust. It was just as well she did, for there was to be no lull for her. In the morning mail she got the proofs of the book she had despatched for Stephen Charteris, after his death. That would be two books published posthumously. They had to be attended to immediately and airmailed back. She shut herself up in the study with them.

So for the next day or two the family saw little of her. They spent a lot of time together, in the drawing-room. They seemed to be having endless discussions over the exciting affair that had ended so satisfactorily. Oh, well, it had certainly been out of the ordinary. The aunts would discuss it for years.

On the Thursday afternoon just after lunch Gareth, his arm out of the sling they'd deemed necessary at first, came into the study, said, 'How near finished are you, Faith? The others don't like you being cooped up as long as this at one sitting.'

'Oh, how sweet of them! I'm used to it. Dad always did the first reading of the proofs, I did the second. I admit I'm a bit weary of it now. I've only got three pages to go, though. Then I'll slip it into its padded envelope, staple it and go into Dunedin with it first thing tomorrow morning so it can catch tomorrow's airmail.'

'We'll all go in. It looks as if they want us at the police station. Mind if I sit here and read, or will I disturb the concentration?'

'Not with so little to finish. As a matter of fact, when it's packed up, I'm going to relax myself in front of this fire.'

He gave her a strange look. 'You aren't, you know. You and I are going to have a serious discussion. If it hadn't been for those blasted proofs, we'd have had it before now.'

The grey eyes went cold. 'Gareth, I could probably give you word for word what you've made up your mind to say. I happened to barge in at the right time in an estate crisis, and you're all handing me more credit than I deserve. You and your stepfather were the ones who took the knocks. I can read you ... you feel under an obligation to me ... to someone you wanted out of the place as fast as she could make it, so you're going to eat humble pie. Well, I don't want you to.

'Nothing is more galling than having to thank someone you wish you'd never set eyes upon. So no discussion, Gareth. *That* would be more than I could take.'

To her astonishment he accepted that meekly. He stretched out his feet to the blaze with every indication of still intending to stay, but said, 'All right, Boadicea, you've cut the legs from under me in the most approved style! And having seen you with that pick-handle the other night, I expect you'll probably swipe me with the fire-irons if I attempt any more grovelling. Please may I stay, Queen of the Iceni?'

She gave him a withering look. 'I don't care whether you go or stay, I just want to finish this.' But the moment it was done, she'd seek the company of the others.

Just as she slid the manuscript into the outsize envelope, he crossed over to the far alcove in search of another book.

Faith got up, took the stapler from the cupboard top, returned to the desk with it. This brought her looking across it to the long French windows.

One could almost believe it was September, and spring, instead of the beginning of August with almost another month of winter to come. There had been a frost, but the sun was striking brilliant blue sparkles from the sea beyond Scimitar Bay; in the neatly pruned rose-bed the drive circled, crocuses were lifting frail golden cups towards its warmth, and alyssum that bloomed all year round here, made purple pools of colour in between their clumps.

She heard the sound of a car. Most cars at Goblin Hill swung round to the back door because it was nearest. She didn't recognise this one as any of the neighbours' cars. Out got a tall figure. There was something familiar about him, but the sun was due north and she couldn't see properly against its brightness. He began to walk round to the front door, must have seen her silhouetted, so stepped smartly up to the windows, tapped, opened them, and stepped in.

'Hullo, Faith darling,' said Glen Tankerville.

Beyond her gasped: '*Glen!*' in a tone of complete consternation, she couldn't say anything. *This was it.* This was where that horrible coil of deceit completely enmeshed her. She felt sick.

Glen didn't look a bit upset at her horrified exclamation. He came across to her, took her hands, said, 'Faith, I know I hurt you, darling, but it was such a shock at first to know you weren't a Charteris. You know what my mother's like—so keen on family. I'm afraid it must have gone very deeply with you when you wouldn't answer my letters. It's so difficult at such a distance. I had to come back to New Zealand for a few weeks anyway. I've just been back two days. It's all right, my love. *I'm* here now to fight your battles and to see you get what's rightfully yours. You've been so much on your own—no one to advise you. But that's all over.

'Mark told me you had no intention of making yourself known to these people. And it *would* be painful for you, at that. But *I'll* do it for you. Mark said he wanted you to have a share of your mother's estate but that you'd refused it. Mind you, I don't think he served you well in that. He ought to have insisted. But then I suppose it meant all the more for him. And now I'm here to be at your side, I'm sure you'll see things in a different light. You were robbed of so much, a name that was rightfully yours, your mother's love, so there ought to be some financial recompense made.'

All Faith could think of was that Gareth was in the alcove, and he'd heard every damaging word. She hadn't been capable of arresting Glen's flow so far. But ... but perhaps what he'd said hadn't been too revealing. He'd not mentioned Julian by name. Except Gareth would know she'd lied about their engagement. She said, putting up a hand, 'Glen, get out of this door this very moment! You've no right in here—none whatever. Just get right out of——'

Gareth's voice cut across hers. 'Faith ... let *me* handle this.' Faith turned, misery breaking over her. Gareth was standing with one hand on the alcove arch looking very confident.

He said, 'Tankerville, I think you're labouring under some apprehension. You don't really think my stepfather wouldn't recognise his own daughter, do you? Why, she's the living image of him and of his Aunt Faith. You don't imagine for a moment we'd let her go away from us? This is her home. She's a Morland and a MacIntyre. She doesn't need her mother's money. That's to go to these institutions Philippa wanted it to go to.

'She has no need of you, Tankerville, either. You let her down badly when you thought she didn't have a name rightfully hers. But you felt quite different when you saw the amount of her mother's estate given in the London papers, didn't you? But Mark had your measure. Faith won't be leaving Goblin Hill. She's marrying *me*, quite soon. There'll always be someone with MacIntyre blood in their veins at Goblin Hill. Mark Denby is coming out here for the wedding. I was speaking to him in London on the phone just this morning.'

He hadn't looked at Faith once in all this time, but she never took her eyes off him. She felt as if everything within her had stilled, as if her brain was numb. Anybody would think *she'd* had a blow on the head. She'd just conjured this up out of an agony of longing. It wasn't happening. It couldn't be.

The door burst open and in came Leonie, a sheaf of papers in her hand. The alcove was opposite the door so she caught sight of her son's figure first. She said, 'Gareth, haven't you finished *yet*? You know how impatient I am to ... Oh, sorry, I didn't know you had anyone here. I didn't hear the bell.'

Her son's voice was very calm, very derisive. 'Oh, he didn't ring, just came straight in. But he's just going.

Mr Tankerville, this is my mother, Mrs Julian Morland. Excuse her interruption. She's just dying to show Faith something.'

Leonie's mouth fell open. She stared. 'Mr Tankerville, did you say? But, Gareth, I don't understand. Why is he——'

Gareth's voice was extremely firm. 'You don't have to understand, Mother. Not right this moment. Oh, good grief, here's Dad now! *And* the whole clan right behind him. Dad, your darling daughter looks as if a brandy would do her good. Will you get her one while I see Mr Tankerville off the premises?'

Mr Tankerville wheeled round, stalked out, got into his rental car, slammed the door and drove off, completely demolishing a clump of alyssum as he took the corner of the rose-bed.

Faith said slowly, as if each word took a great effort to produce, 'I—don't—want a brandy—but I—think I'd like —to sit down.'

She subsided on to the arm of the big old study chair by the fire, closed her eyes, then opened them to see them all regarding her, smilingly.

'I'm first!' burst out of Julian Morland, and reaching her, he gathered her into his arms. When Faith raised her head, she saw tears slipping down Leonie's cheeks and knew them for tears of joy. She went to her next, very naturally.

She was bewildered, laughing, happy ... and she wouldn't meet Gareth's eyes. He had said ... he had said ... they were getting married ... *he knew who she was and he didn't mind!* It was too much for a girl to take in.

Robert said, 'I was so pleased when you called me Robert, love, but there's another name I'd sooner hear you use than any.'

She smiled shakily, said, 'Grandfather!' and reached out to enfold Prudence too, 'Gran ... oh, Gran, but I said it once before and you thought it was a slip from hearing Gareth say it.'

'I didn't,' said Prudence, her purply-pansy eyes shining like a young girl's, 'I knew it for real. I've known ever since Leonie rang me from Arizona and pretended it was because of the twins' birthday.'

Hope and Chassie were just about dying of frustration, but now Hope got in, 'And as soon as Leonie told her who you were and said that above all things we had to keep you here by sheer force if necessary, till they got home, Prudence tore upstairs to look in your trinket-case to see if you had a pendant to match the earrings you were wearing.'

Faith blinked. 'But what's that got to do with anything?'

Chassie got in this time. 'Your mother must have given them to you. She did, didn't she? Yes, well, they'd been our Faith's. Harold had given them to her. They came to Prudence and she gave them to Julian for Philippa. She must have wanted them to go to you, and rightly so.'

'She gave them to me for my twenty-first. She didn't tell me, of course, and I knew they were antique, but she had a lot of jewellery like that. I expect that was one of the things she forgot to tell me when she was—in those last few weeks.'

Leonie said almost fiercely, 'I'm so glad she called you Faith. I so longed to give Julian a daughter called that, a son called Duncan. Oh, it's just wonderful!'

Faith said, 'Look, let's go into the drawing-room. There's more room there for everyone to sit down. There are so many things I must ask. I'd no idea——'

Leonie said, 'We were going to tell you the day after the mutton-poaching, only that happened and upset things and then you got that wretched lot of proofs to do. We were going to do it gently. I'd had this wonderful idea ... I wrote it out as an ending to the history. Julian finding his daughter. And I was just coming in to give it to you now when I found that Glen Tankerville here. I still don't know quite what happened.'

Faith said imploringly, 'Do let's get out of here and sit down and sort it out ... I'm so dizzy with happiness I can't take anything in.' She still wouldn't look fully at Gareth. This was the time for her father, for her step-mother, her aunts, her grandparents.

She thought Gareth had got carried away by the fact that she'd saved the situation as far as the sheep-stealing went and Glen's coming had gone to his head. He'd made a grand gesture, that was all. She must give him time to cool off.

Prudence said, 'I'll have to just dash along to the kitchen and turn the oven down. I left the casserole on high. I made the pudding this morning so we wouldn't have to stop in the middle of the explanations, but I mustn't burn the casserole. But don't start till I get back.'

They all hurried along the hall and stopped dead in their tracks as the doorbell rang furiously. Gareth craned his neck to look out of the glass side-panel and said in a tone of horror, 'It's the law ... with a fistful of papers! Now we'll never get it told!' They all collapsed into help-less laughter. Then Robert pulled himself together and opened the door.

The police officer looked slightly amazed at this solid block of people who'd apparently all rushed to welcome him in.

'Had to be in Palmerston,' he said cheerfully, 'so I thought a few papers could be signed. Could facilitate the preparatory work for the court. We want a few things corroborated too.'

Faith clutched Gareth, who was nearest her. 'See if you can whisper to Dad not to say I'm his daughter, because if I have to sign anything, it'll look funny being Charteris and it'll be far too complicated to explain. And, Gareth, I realise you just got carried away just now—I mean about this marriage business. Don't say anything about that in front of the family—it certainly rocked Glen, and I'm most grateful. But we can discuss it later.'

His lips twitched. 'We sure will. We'll do other things later too, like fixing a wedding date. Do you realise how self-sacrificing I was when Dad claimed first kiss, damn it? Don't worry about the family. *They* planned it. Now go in, idiot, and stop havering. That chap's got a job to do.'

When they finally got into the drawing-room Faith gazed in surprise at the really lavish afternoon tea spread out on a lace-cloth. The silver tea-service was out, the silver scone-basket. There were sandwiches, cream kisses, melting moments, lamingtons. The police officer's eyes positively glistened. 'I say, I'm not interrupting anything, am I? That almost looks like a birthday party!'

Leonie said hastily, 'Oh, it's not that, just that it's not often we're all together at once. We thought we'd do it in style today. The kettle's boiled. We were just waiting for my son and stepdaughter to join us. They were in the study busy on some manuscripts—a family history. It's a joint effort on their part—it's taken months and it's just completed.'

Well, Gareth hadn't had time to warn his mother, but the policeman didn't suspect involved family relations and said nothing. Leonie said, 'You'd love to join us, wouldn't you? You must get called out on the most horrible jobs, so it'd be a nice change to relax for a few moments, wouldn't it?' She beamed on him.

'Here we go,' said Gareth, in Faith's ear. 'Trust my mother! We'll be here till dinner—I know it. After me having to play second fiddle to Stephen Charteris's proofs, I've still got everything bottled up inside me. I've just got rid of one complex and I'm developing another! Talk about rotten timing! The only thing I've enjoyed so far was throwing Glen Tankerville out on his ear. It was a wonderful moment. After Mark Denby told me on the phone how he'd treated you, I was almost hoping he'd refuse to go so I could really get at him. I——' The policeman cleared his throat and started in on the law business.

All of a sudden Faith was perfectly sure it was going to

be all right. Leonie came back with the teapot, poured. The great-aunts did it all beautifully, handing cakes and sandwiches round, drawing out the policeman to talk about himself, his wife, his family.

'I knew it,' said Gareth. He was speaking into Faith's ear from where he sat on the arm of her chair. 'In a moment he'll be bringing out photos of his children. Faith, if Gran gets all carried away too and asks if he'd like dinner with us on his way back from Palmerston, I'll kill her. Faith, remember your manners ... don't get the giggles now. Oh, I see!'

The policeman was unbuttoning his jacket and drawing out photos. He was sweet. 'There are eight of us to pass them round,' whispered Gareth, despairingly. Everyone made suitable responses. Only Faith's and Gareth's were feeble. They were the only two who knew that the really important busines had still to be settled.

Faith was almost overcome at the look on Gareth's face when the aunts and her grandmother even dived off to get the man a carton of eggs, a couple of chickens from the deep freeze and then stood farewelling him and telling him to be sure to bring his wife and children out to the beach when the weather was warmer. Finally they waved him off.

Gareth shut the verandah door firmly, said, 'Right, does anyone know where we got to? Look, I'd like to sweep Faith off right now, but I'm inclined to think she'll raise a lot of objections to—to certain things unless she gets everybody else's reactions first, so lead on.'

Prudence said anxiously, 'Haven't you any idea what the time is? That casserole had been on high too long as it was, even though I added boiling water. The explanations are going to take hours. Do you think everyone could brush up, and we could talk as we eat?'

Robert said, 'Prue, couldn't you switch it off and heat it later? It wouldn't matter if we didn't eat till eight.'

Prudence looked a bit guilty. 'Well, you see when we knew Faith would be through the proofs by afternoon tea-time, we thought everything would be settled long since ... and I got Hope and Chassie to ring their daughters and they and their husbands are coming down from Oamaru tonight. They'll be here by eight and will have had their dinners.'

Gareth took one horrified look at her, then at Faith. He clutched the stair-post and guffawed. 'I can't stand it ... they've done everything too soon. I expect you told them you'd have some interesting news for them? Did you? You did? I just can't stand it!'

Faith came to. 'Well, you'll jolly well have to, Gareth Morgan. They're my family, and what my family wants they get. Upstairs and change. That's what you want us to do, isn't it, Gran? Right. Off you go!' She ran up after him, laughing.

She opened the door of her room and stopped dead, one hand still on the handle. On a tiny table near the window stood a crystal vase with the first of the snowdrops in it. Snowdrops ... She heard someone behind her and turned. It was her father. He swept her inside and shut the door, turned the old-fashioned key.

His gaze was on the snowdrops too, meaningly. She looked at him uncertainly.

He said, 'Yes, love, I put them there when you went back to the study after lunch. You may not know, but they were your mother's favourite flowers. It was one of those little quirks of personality that I found so endearing in her. You'd expect so colourful a person to adore orchids, or lilies, or big flamboyant roses, but she didn't. She liked these pale shy snowdrops, hiding away under the trees in the far corner of the garden.'

Faith's eyes were full of tears. 'Dad, I did know. I must show you.'

She went across to her bedside table, picked up her diary, opened it at that page that recorded how she and her mother had walked in that Surrey garden and Philippa had found that first snowdrop and had made a covenant with her.

Julian Morland touched it gently. 'We'll both think of Pippa every spring.' He looked at her, then at the snowdrops in her vase. 'I did so want your mother to share a little in our joy today.' He put his arms around her, drew her close, put his cheek against hers and went out.

It crowned Faith's day.

Everyone had changed into festive attire. What a good-looking family, Faith exulted, sitting at the round table with her father on one side, Gareth on the other, next to his mother.

She had changed into a long lavender-blue skirt, with a wide-necked tunic top above it in hydrangea colours, smudgy blues and purples and rose. Philippa had bought it for her. It had cost the earth and looked it. The amethyst pendant glowed on Faith's brown skin, the matching earrings swung from her ears; her light brown hair, curling in tendrils on her wide creamy brow, shone in the candlelight.

Prudence said, 'It may be only a casserole dinner, but at least we can have it with glamour. Hope and Chassie unearthed those rose-coloured candles.' Pale rosé wine glowed in the goblets, firelight winked in the polished silver, and in tiny white vases were the primroses and violets of that long-ago Faith's planting, that those two dear sentimental great-aunts had brought up from the Hansel-and-Gretel Wood earlier in the day.

Hope said, 'At our age one is so grateful for candlelight.'

Charity nodded. 'There was a poem our mother used to say whenever we had dinner by candlelight. I think I can remember only a couple of lines:

'For candlelight is merciful and candlelight is kind
  To eyes the years have faded and cheeks that time
    has lined ...'

Faith felt she could almost hear Olivia saying it, see her across the table, her dark-gold hair piled high, the pansy-purply eyes alight with joy because a MacIntyre still carried on at Goblin Hill. Prudence dished her casserole.

Julian said, eyes alight, 'It wouldn't matter what we ate tonight. It would be ambrosia and nectar. You know ... a loaf of bread, a jug of wine ...'

Faith turned to him. 'Oh, Father, you *are* like Dad. *He* used to say things like that,' and they all burst out laughing. She added, 'How lucky can a girl get? To have a father, a foster-father and a stepfather! And all such wonderful people.'

Julian said unsteadily, 'The first toast we'll drink to-night will be to Stephen and Lucy Charteris who kept my darling safe and happy, till she could come home.'

Gareth's hand sought Faith's under the deep overhang of the snowy-white linen cloth Euphemia MacIntyre had brought with her from Scotland a hundred and twenty years before. His touch gave Faith confidence.

She said, 'There's still an awful lot of explaining to do. Will someone please begin? If Mark told my father and Leonie, then you'll know my side of it. How I didn't know till after Stephen died that I was adopted, then went to England still not knowing, to ask my godmother who my parents were. And that I decided to come here just to see you all and to go away again. Oh, how glad I am that I wrote and told Mark all about it, seeing that made him go to see you and Leonie, Father.'

Julian shook his head. 'Not the two of us. Just one—Leonie. He felt she must be the one to decide what to do.'

Gareth said soberly, 'That was because of me and my stupid complex.'

Faith said, 'Your very understandable complex. Not for yourself, but for your mother.'

Leonie acknowledged that with a grateful look at her son. 'I was *never* jealous of Philippa. She belonged to Julian's youth. The Julian I fell in love with wasn't that

Julian at all. And he made it very clear to me how much I meant to him.'

'And rightly so,' said Faith.

Leonie continued, 'All I wanted to do when Mark told me was to get home, but we'd promised to visit so many folk. When we rang here, I made Faith promise to stay till we got here, then rang when I was on my own, to tell Mother. Then I telescoped the visits. Julian thought I was getting homesick and liked the idea. I didn't tell him because I had this feeling that I wanted him to get to know Faith first, so he'd have no apprehensions about meeting her. I thought if she was one quarter as nice as her grandparents and great-aunts said, to say nothing of Gareth, then he was bound to like her for herself alone.'

Julian took it up. 'I'm glad she did it that way, but it nearly killed her, keeping that secret. She'd really have liked to tie you up with blue ribbons and present you to me, Faith. But she didn't know how to tell Gareth, or how to tell you she knew. Then she got this idea of writing it out as an ending to the book and giving it to you to read.' He started to laugh. 'And it came unstuck, about five minutes too soon, with Glen arriving. Faith, Leonie had told me that night, before I saw the poachers' lights. Of course she'd not quite written to the end of the final chapter because she dared not throw in the wedding of her son to my daughter ... because she still hadn't told Gareth. That was the fly in the ointment.'

Faith looked up at Gareth, said, 'I don't know yet why you're not more furious than ever. Remember how you were when you thought I'd come here out of idle curiosity because I happened to be Philippa's daughter?'

The way he looked down on her they could have been alone in a world of their own. The others watched, enchanted. He said, 'That's so completely different. Coming here to your father's home, *your* home, was the most natural thing in the world.'

Faith caught in a breath, released it on a sigh, said, 'I expect that's masculine logic. I like it even if I'll never understand it. I'll never, never forget my feelings when Glen walked in. I thought he'd be thrown out and me after him. It was terrible of me to use him like that. To say I was spoken for. Because I never answered any of his letters after the first. But when *did* Leonie tell you, Gareth?'

His face crinkled into laughter lines. 'She didn't. She had it all planned for the day after the mutton-poaching. Dad had left her finishing her chapter for the very last time when he came down to get me. So I found out myself.'

Faith looked amazed. 'How could you?'

'I've a confession to make, Faith. I wasn't knocked out, just winded. And you knelt by your father and said, "Dad, Dad, are you all right?"'

Faith swung to look at her father. He nodded. 'I heard it, but I knew. So I pretended I was out to it too. Go on, Gareth.'

Gareth grinned. 'I thought I was hearing things! After all, I had a knock on the head. But it must have stimulated me, cleared my brain. It absolutely flashed upon me—a moment of truth. Your name ... your two Christian names ... your likeness to Dad in colouring. Your parents close friends of Philippa's. It's a wonder I didn't black right out. Especially the next moment when you leaned over me and said what you did ... a girl who was supposed to be marrying someone else ... and muttering endearments over my apparently senseless form!'

'Ohhhhhh!' said Faith, remembering.

Her father burst out laughing. 'It's all right, Faith, I won't let him repeat it. Don't forget I heard it too. But I'd realised before that you'd just used Glen as a smoke-screen because of Gareth. What a family! Talk about getting in a tizzy. Oh, well, the MacIntyres were aye like that. Their very motto is *Per ardua*. Through difficulties. I think it applies to most of us.'

Gareth said, 'That's an incomplete motto. It ought to read *Per ardua ad astra*. Through labour to the stars.'

His eyes met Faith's as they looked up at him. 'This time we've reached the stars.'

More happy sighs from the whole company.

Julian continued, 'Of course Mark told Leonie there was no chance of you marrying Glen, that you'd turned him down before you went to England, and why. But she was very worried for a while after getting home. Apparently, despite that sedative, Gareth tossed and turned all night after the fracas. But during those hours he pieced the whole thing together. He nearly went mad next morning when those proofs came in. But once you got settled with them, he called a family conclave. He was most amazed when he found half of us knew already. He told us of his unfortunate remarks about his matchmaking family at your first meeting, so that explained this bogus engagement to Glen. But he was still puzzled about a conversation he'd overheard you making. He'd thought it had supplied conclusive proof that you did care for that bounder. But your grandmother cleared that one up.'

'She did? How?'

Gareth said, 'Well, you've guessed that it was when you were speaking to Mark. I jumped to the conclusion that it was Glen and you deliberately let me believe it. I could beat you for it! But remember my mother rang that night to speak to Gran, and Gran had a little conversation with Jess Gilchrist, the operator, till it came through?'

'Yes?'

'Jess said to her, "Well, for a Sleepy Hollow village we've had an exciting day. First a ring from Hollywood for Goblin Hill, and now one from Phoenix, Arizona. How International can we get? And to think it was Philippa Meredith's husband. Her producer!" At that moment Leonie's call came through. I don't suppose Jess ever knew about Philippa and her connection here, and as the call was for a Miss Faith Charteris, didn't connect it with the family. Leonie's call explained it all for Mother, of course, seeing she'd seen Mark and now was explaining who Faith was.'

Leonie said, 'And then after Mother being so good, I was the one who nearly blew it when I mentioned knowing about the end of *The Pengarths of the Cove*.'

Gareth said, laughing, 'When I think of the way Faith let me go on thinking she was planning a honeymoon in the Lake District and Scotland, I think it's very magnanimous of me to marry her at all.'

Faith pulled a face. 'Nobody asked you to. Come to think of it, *you* haven't asked *me* yet! You just brazenly announced to Glen that we were getting married.'

'I never am going to ask you. You'll be the one MacIntyre woman who won't be able to tell her grandchildren how Grandpapa proposed! And you're not even having the privilege of choosing your own engagement ring. You're having the first Faith's one—an amethyst one that matches the earrings. Your grandfather cleaned it with meths earlier this afternoon! But——No, Aunt Hope, she is not having another helping of apricots. No, Aunt Chassie, we won't be staying for coffee. Don't you realise I've not even kissed my fiancée yet? Come on, wench, I've had enough of this. Off to the study with you ...'

Willingly, she complied, but turned at the door to see that ring of dear faces illumined by firelight and candlelight. Happy, happy faces, and Leonie's happiest of all.

'We'll be back soon, dear family,' she said wickedly.

The study fire still glowed redly to its heart. One standard lamp was on by the desk. The heavy curtains were drawn, shutting out the dark shadow of the recumbent, benevolent goblin and the never-ending song of the sea.

'Soon wasn't the right word, sweetheart,' said Gareth Morgan. 'This hour is ours alone. Now ... are you going to make the waiting worth while?'

His arms enfolded her. He bent his head ...

Welcome to the Wonderful World of Harlequin Books

Dear Reader:

We hope you enjoyed reading this compelling Harlequin romance novel.

Thanks to your support, Harlequins have become the most popular romances in the United States, in Canada and throughout the world.

Watch for them in your favorite store — there's lots more entertaining reading ahead.

Harlequin Romances

A unique series of special Harlequins featuring such great authors as Violet Winspear, Anne Hampson, Rachel Lindsay, Anne Mather, Rosalind Brett and many more.

Four new Presents are issued each month and feature thrilling stories set in enchanting locations vividly described by Harlequin's most popular authors.

They are too good to miss. Buy them at your local store. Or, fill in the coupon on the last page of this section for details on how to have them delivered to your home.

Harlequin Presents...

Harlequin MAGAZINE

The newest idea in the Harlequin repertoire of romance fiction. North America's enchantingly different magazine created by the same people who bring you Harlequin Romances and Harlequin Presents books.

Monthly issues contain

- a full-length romantic novel
- a Harlequin author's own story
- a travel article
- delicious recipes
- readers' letters
- short stories
- puzzle contest and much more

This magazine is not sold in stores. For further information, please fill in the following coupon.

Fill in and Mail this Coupon Today!